SARA'S
TREK

Florence Schloneger

ress

N   ansas

Library of Congress Number 81-71093
International Standard Book Number 0-87303-071-0
Printed in the United States of America
Copyright © 1981 by Faith and Life Press
718 Main Street, Newton, Kansas 67114

Illustrated by Sidney Quinn
Design by John Hiebert
Printing by Mennonite Press, Inc.

Faith and
Life Press

For Nettie Bergmann who was
willing to share her story.

CHAPTER 1

Planes screeched over the Polish countryside, and the January air was thick with the smoke of their bombs. The earth trembled and shuddered as giant tanks rumbled over the snowy ground, and the constant throbbing of the guns seemed to say, "Coming, coming, the war is coming to Wulka."

"Hitch up the wagon, Franz," Papa said, his voice tense with anxiety. "Sara, get some potatoes. We have to get out of here."

Sara Friesen turned, nearly tripping over her long legs, and hurried to her bedroom. The potatoes could wait. She was not going to be cold *this* time if she could help it! Her hands fumbled as she pulled on her striped woolen stockings and tied them up with strings. She threaded the frayed twine shoestring up her boot. Hurriedly she pulled on a shabby coat that was clearly too small for a tall eleven-year-old and stuffed a woolen scarf in her pocket. Then she ran to the storeroom, grabbed a full bucket of potatoes in each hand, and staggered out into the cold morning air toward the wagon.

"Hurry," Papa said impatiently, lifting his forefinger to flick the frost from his graying mustache. He lifted the buckets into the wagon, and Sara scrambled in.

Mama brought a pile of blankets, holding the top of the pile in place with her chin. She put them in the wagon, scanned the eastern sky, and hurried back for another load. Twenty-year-old Marga came with a big iron kettle stacked full of a few necessary dishes, and by the time Mama returned with several suitcases, the small wagon was almost full. Franz climbed aboard the driver's seat, pulled the flap of his fur-lined cap over his ears, and slapped the reins against the scrawny horse. Papa, Mama, and Marga followed on foot.

Sara sat in the wagon, watching the Polish farmhouse she had called home for nine months disappear in the distance. "Here we go again," she sighed. She lay back on the pile of blankets and looked up at the tin roof over her head, remembering. Papa had added the roof to the wagon over a year ago when the war had forced them to leave their home in Steinfeld, Russia. It had rained and sleeted almost the whole trip. Sara still remembered how the wheels grew thick with mud, and her clothes had stiffened with hardened slime. No wonder they had all gotten lice. Just thinking about them made her head itch. Papa had finally cropped off her long, brown hair, but it had gradually grown back. Last week she had been able to form a short braid again. She drew her coat tighter, closed her eyes, and tried to forget.

Sara could tell by the increasing noise that they must have turned onto a main road. There was the steady rhythm of horses' hooves, the creak of hundreds of wagons, and the step and clump of boots in all sizes and shapes. She sat up and looked out the back of the wagon. The road was jammed with people fleeing west, their wagons piled high with belongings. Behind the traveling crowd, Sara could hear the artillery and see red flames leaping into the gray winter sky.

"A plane, a plane!" someone screamed, and the desperate refugees pushed and shoved to get off the road. Suddenly there was a loud explosion, and dirt went flying in all directions. Sara ducked as a stone flew past her and landed in a bucket of potatoes. She leaned over to pick it up, but when she straightened to throw it out, the road was already a solid mass of people and wagons so that it was impossible to tell where the bomb had landed.

Papa appeared at the back of the wagon. "I'm tired," he said, flinching with pain as a rasping cough shook his body. "Could you get off and let me ride for awhile?" Sara jumped down, and Papa climbed aboard with great effort and flopped back on the blankets.

"Hey, Sara!" a familiar voice called.

Sara turned quickly, scanning the crowd to see who was calling her. When she saw a young girl running through the traffic, long blond braids flying behind her, she squealed with delight, "Liese! (Le'suh) You're on the trek again too!"

Liese Rempel had been her next-door neighbor back in Russia. They had often spent summer afternoons running through the fields, picking wild flowers, and playing house in the shade of the acacia trees. Liese's family, too, had been part of the long trek to Poland last winter and had settled on a farm about two kilometers from Wulka.

Liese pulled her braids in front of her shoulders and immediately took charge. Sara relaxed—when Liese was around, things happened. They linked arms, and Liese pulled her on ahead of the wagon.

"Don't go too far ahead," Marga called after them. That was just like Marga—she always had taken care of Sara because Mama had worked long hours every day, milking cows at the commune in Russia.

"We won't," Sara replied, waving at the tall, thin figure. Even the dark woolen scarf couldn't hide Marga's black, wavy hair, and it only drew attention to the large eyes that dominated her narrow face.

There was shelter in the fleeing crowd. The horses and wagons formed a barrier that shut out the sight of advancing fire and smoke, and the clip-clop of hooves nearly drowned out the booming guns and screeching planes.

Liese practiced marching, kicking her feet up high and straight like the German soldiers. Sara joined in, but when Liese hung onto the back of a wagon, she became afraid and skipped along behind instead.

"I'm tired," Sara said, finally. "Let's stop."

"We can't, silly," Liese said. "We're running away from the Russians."

Sara became quiet, and a shiver ran down her back. She wished Papa was stronger so that she could ride. Her legs ached, and she was starting to get cold. Even the horses were tired. The sound of slapping reins increased with the lengthening day, and the yelling of the drivers became louder and more desperate.

When the caravan finally stopped, the sun had set, leaving streaks of pink and orange over the western sky. Marga left to find water, and Mama started cutting up potatoes. Papa took a few bricks out of the wagon, stacked them for a makeshift fireplace, and sent Sara to find sticks. All she could find were the broken boards of a shattered wagon, but the heavy wood made a roaring fire. When Marga returned with water from a nearby stream, they soon had a boiling pot of potato soup.

Beside them, a young mother was hanging diapers on the side of her wagon. Sara knew that by morning they would be frozen stiff and that the mother would probably put them against her body to warm them. She shivered at the very thought of it and sat down near the fire on an upside-down bucket to get warm.

Mama handed her a dish of soup, and Sara ate slowly, letting the piping hot broth trickle down her throat. She let her body sit heavily on the overturned bucket, glad to rest her aching feet and feel the friendly warmth of the fire.

Marga broke the silence. "What do you think is going to happen?" she asked in a hollow voice. "Will the Russians catch up with us?"

Papa coughed. "Doesn't look too good," he said, rubbing his unshaven face, "but if we can make it into Germany we should be all right."

"Yes," Franz chimed in with sixteen-year-old confidence as he brushed his blond hair out of his eyes. "We can count on Germany to stop those dumb 'Ruskies' sooner or later."

Germany! Yes, there they would be all right. Sara liked the Germans. She had only been seven when Germany's Hitler with his army of three million troops had defeated the Russian Communists. How the Mennonites had rejoiced! For as long as Sara could remember, their church building had been used by the Communists as a movie theater. But when the Germans came it had been reopened for worship, and she had gone to Sunday school for the first time. She had sat with wide-eyed wonder, listening to everyone singing "Gott ist die Liebe," and marveled that they all seemed to know something she had never heard before. But it didn't take long until she could sing it as lustily as the rest.

It wasn't only Sundays that were different. The whole atmosphere seemed more free. The Communists had hated her people. Papa once said it was because the Mennonites were so rich. Sara hadn't known any rich Mennonites, but she did call the most beautiful farms by such Mennonite names as Reimer, Unrau, Redekop, and Cornies. Those farms had all been divided into collectives and the men taken away to prison or concentration camps. But after the Germans came, in 1943, families were no longer moved off their farms or the fathers taken away.

Then last year the Communist army had gained in strength and driven the Germans out of Russia. Sara's family and many other Mennonites had fled to Poland with the retreating Germans. They knew the Russians would see them as traitors because of their Low German language and democratic ideas. But now it was January 1945. They were no longer safe in Poland either because the Russian army was advancing and taking over Poland as well.

Sara stood up, stretched her aching muscles, and went to get a blanket in the wagon. Germany. If only they could get to Germany they would be all right. She crawled under the wagon, rolled up in the blanket, and tried to sleep.

The morning was still a dull gray when Sara wakened to the throbbing hum of airplanes and the shuffling sounds of hundreds of people preparing to move. Franz was already hitching up the horse. Sara rolled over, feeling as stiff as a piece of frozen canvas. "Come on," Papa called. "We have to get...." A harsh cough interrupted. He spat on the ground, leaving a bloody stain.

"Not again," Sara thought. That could only mean that Papa was worse. Even in Russia, he hadn't been strong enough to farm like other men, but he had gotten weaker during the long winter trek from Russia.

She stood up, folded her blanket, and threw it into the wagon. The cold night had left her body sluggish and so numb that when she blew on her fingers and rubbed them against her cheek they felt like rubber. Franz clucked to the horse, and Sara had no choice but to follow the wagon, moving her stiff legs back and forth automatically.

Mama fell in step beside her. "Cold?" she asked with concern. She pulled a piece of dark rye bread from the pocket of her long dark coat and handed it to Sara. "This will have to be your breakfast," she said with a sigh. Her mouth closed in a straight line and her tired eyes looked ahead at the never-ending road. Liese filtered out of the crowd and joined them again, but even she was quiet and tense with cold, and they walked on in silence.

The morning brightened as it started to snow. Now their woolen scarves were covered with a layer of white, and their breath formed puffs of steam in the chilly air.

Suddenly a blast of horns sent the crowd scurrying. People

yelled, horses whinnied, and wagons creaked as everyone tried to get off the road. Sara scrambled into the ditch and turned to see a line of German army jeeps crawl out of the snowy landscape. But Franz was still on the road, pulling hard at the reins as he tried to hold the rearing, pawing horse. Mama cautiously approached it, patting its side. She managed to grab the harness, but the wagon lurched over a deep rut and toppled. Sara heard the potatoes bang against the tin roof and saw them roll out over the snowy ground. The driver of the leading jeep jumped out and waved his arms frantically. "Get this thing off the road!" he shouted. He motioned to the other soldiers in the jeep, and soon they lifted it and pushed it off the road.

Luckily, most of the potatoes had rolled into the ditch, so Sara started picking them up. But long after they were all gathered in the buckets, the jeeps were still coming.

"I'm freezing," Liese said, trying to escape the wind by standing behind a solitary pine tree. "Let's walk ahead."

"Yes, they'll catch up with us after a while," Sara said with a shiver.

As they walked, the houses became closer together. Ahead of them a steeple stood at attention, watching over hundreds of snowy rooftops. Beside them a picket fence lined the street. Sara looked longingly at a lone curl of smoke rising from a chimney. "I wonder what's taking them so long," she said.

They walked on, trying to fight off the cold that blasted at their backs and grabbed at their legs. Sara let her hand drag across the

top of the fence, brushing away the snow. "They're sure taking a long time," she said for the second time, feeling suddenly weak.

"Let's go back," Liese said.

Sara hadn't realized they had come so far. They walked faster now. Her side ached, and the cold cut into her lungs. Finally when she could see the lone pine tree, she started to run. Her breath came in heavy gasps, and a terrible knot of pain tightened within her. The wagon and the people were gone! Desperately she looked around—perhaps this wasn't the place after all. Then her toe bumped a potato, and she knew—this was the place. Tears welled up and trickled down her cheek. Slowly she picked up the potato and put it in her pocket.

CHAPTER 2

"Come on, let's go back to town—maybe they passed us," Liese said, starting to run. Sara glanced around and followed, leaving a crying wail behind in the winter air.

Soon they were in town again—passing the fences, the steeple, and the snow-covered houses. A woman approached them in the street. "What's wrong?" she asked gently.

"We . . . we can't find our parents," Liese replied.

"Where did you come from?" she asked.

"Wulka."

"I don't think we can find them in this confusion," she said, putting an arm around each of them. "I'll give you something to eat, and then we'll decide what to do."

A few minutes later, Sara sat in a cheery room holding a clean handkerchief and licking thick, yellow jam from a piece of bread. It was then that she noticed the Red Cross patch on the woman's sleeve. "I wish I could stay with you," the nurse told them, "but I've just been informed that everyone in town has to leave. The Russians are very close, and I must pass the word along. I think the best thing for you to do is to go to the train station. Everyone will be waiting there for the evacuation."

"But what about our parents?" Liese asked desperately.

"There's not time to find them," the lady said quietly. "They've probably had to move on, too. You *must* go to the train station."

Sara began to cry. "But how do we know where the station is?" she sobbed.

"Come on, Sara," said Liese, "we can make it!"

"I'll come with you part of the way," the woman reassured them. "It isn't hard to find."

The girls followed her down the street. "I have to go now," she said after they had walked for several minutes. "Take this street straight west for four blocks and wait at the station. There will be a lot of people waiting—just get on the train. I'm sorry I can't stay with you." She waved good-bye and walked away in the opposite direction.

The girls walked hurriedly down the street. There it was—the railroad station. Sara pulled open the heavy door and stepped inside. The place was deserted. Where were all the people? Where was the train?

"Oh, no," Sara said desperately. "The train's left without us."

"Let's see if we can catch the Red Cross nurse again," Liese said, starting to run.

At least Liese knew what to do, Sara thought, and followed her. They raced down the street, past the square where they had last seen her, and beyond. Finally, they saw a long line of army trucks ahead, and Liese ran after them. "Take us along!" she yelled.

"What's your trouble?" a driver yelled out, stopping his truck.

"May we go with you?" Liese asked.

"No, but if you go to the train station, they'll take you," he answered.

"But no one was there," Sara protested.

"Well, they should be by now. You must have been the first ones," he said, and moved on.

They turned and ran again. This time when they arrived at the station, it was full. They paused a moment, looking around.

"Let's stay by her," Sara whispered, pointing to a woman with a baby and a small child. "She looks nice."

Liese walked boldly up to her. "May we go with you?" she asked.

"Oh, yes," the woman said with a relieved look. "I need someone to help with Maria. I'm so worried she'll toddle off and get lost in the crowd. I can't hold onto her with a suitcase in one hand and a baby in the other."

Maria lowered her head and grabbed her mother's skirts, then peeked up at Sara with large, curious eyes. Just then the roar of an approaching train sent the crowd into a frenzy. Sara grabbed Maria's hand and stood as close as she could to the woman. Liese picked up the suitcase. Together they edged their way through the crowd. The cars filled rapidly, and one after another their heavy doors slammed shut. Sara grabbed the woman's dress and

followed so closely that she stepped on her heels. They *had* to get on! Maria was crying and pulling hard to free herself, but Sara held her hand tightly and pulled her along through the slow-moving mob.

"There's room up here!" Liese shouted, clambering aboard the last car. She reached down to help the others on board.

"Thank you," the woman sighed with relief when they were settled on the hard floor of the boxcar. "I could never have managed alone." In the semidarkness, Sara could see tears glisten in her eyes.

Next morning they were still sitting in the same confined positions. Painful hunger cramps and dry lips reminded Sara that it had been a long time since she had eaten. Besides, the crowded quarters didn't allow room to stretch her long legs or rest her aching back, and she was tired.

The train slowed to a crawl, then stopped with a jerk. "Now's our chance!" a young man yelled. "Anyone have containers we can gather snow in? We have to get drinking water."

He opened the door, letting in a flood of light. Four lunch buckets appeared, were quickly filled, and the door slammed shut again, leaving them in darkness until their eyes could readjust to the dim light.

The man set the buckets on the stove in the middle of the car to melt the snow, then passed the water around, carefully measuring the amount in a tin cup so that everybody got some.

It was after Sara had a drink that she remembered the potato. She dug into her pocket and carefully brought out the hard brown vegetable. She rubbed it on her coat, then took a bite, slowly savoring its faint tartness.

"What do you have there?" Liese asked, hearing the crunching sound of chewing.

Sara quickly put the potato back into her pocket. It was hers!

"Please, I'm so hungry," Liese begged.

Sara looked at her, fingering the potato's rough skin. Liese did look hungry. "Here," she said finally, "you take a bite and then I'll take one."

"Mmm," Liese said, taking the potato eagerly, "best potato I ever tasted."

The train suddenly braked and sent them sliding toward the front. The door was shoved open from the outside by a red-faced soldier. "The track's blown up!" he shouted. "You can't go any farther." He hitched his rucksack over his shoulders and started to run. "The Russians are close!" he called back. ". . . be here any minute."

The train emptied quickly, and Sara stood in a daze watching the panicky crowd scatter like leaves in a gust of wind. She moved closer to the lady who cradled her small baby in one hand and stroked Maria's head with the other. "I'm not running," the young mother said softly. "I can't." She moved slowly toward a nearby house, trying to walk with Maria clinging to her leg.

Liese grabbed Sara's hand. "Come on," she said in a high-pitched voice. Sara stood still, looking blankly after the lady and her children. Liese's eyes flashed angrily. "Well, if you don't want to run, you don't have to," she said in disgust, "but I'm not staying here for those Russians to get me."

Sara looked toward the east. Billows of black smoke darkened the sky. The Russians were close, all right. She swallowed a sob and started to run after Liese.

Her side hurt, her breath came in short gasps, and her long legs stumbled over the uneven ground. Still she ran.

"Look," Liese gasped, pointing to an open boxcar. Its cargo had been plundered by the frantic mob, and tins of fish were scattered over the ground. Sara stopped and picked up several of the ice cold cans. A wooden barrel with a smashed top caught her attention—butter! She poked at it, but it was frozen solid. She picked up a stick, dug into the mass of yellow, and put a piece in her pocket.

Then they ran again. Sara ran until her tired legs refused and she had to slow to a frantic walk. Ahead of them a truckload of German soldiers stopped briefly. "Here's our chance to get a ride," Liese shouted. "Hop on." Sara lunged forward just as the truck started up with a jerk, grabbed the tailgate, and hung on. "Don't let go of your fish," Liese shouted above the roar of the motor.

"Hey, stop!" one of the soldiers yelled. "We got two little girls hanging on the back." The truck slowed to a stop, and he pulled them aboard. Sara sat down heavily on the truck bed, letting the wheels propel her on and on and on, away from the Russians.

By mid-afternoon the truck stopped in front of a small store, and a soldier hopped off and went in. The smell of fresh bread filled the air. Sara's mouth watered, and she reached into her pocket for the frozen butter and the tins of fish. Oh, they were cold! Her fingers ached, and her toes felt numb. If only she could go inside and get warm.

The soldier returned with a loaf of bread, broke it in pieces, and passed it around. Sara held it in her open palm, enjoying its steaming freshness, then reached into her pocket for a bit of butter. She wrapped it in the soft bread, hoping the warmth would soften it, then took a bite. Even cold butter seemed like a treat.

"Will you share your fish?" one of the soldiers asked. He reached into his pocket, pulled out a jackknife, and flipped out a can opener. "You first," he said as he cut the tin. Sara picked out a stiff fish and bit into the icy flesh. It numbed her throat and she shivered, but she reached out for a second piece.

It was now that Sara noticed two women in the front of the truck. One was tall and thin with lovely black hair hanging around a stern, tense face. The other woman was shorter. Her blond hair was drawn back into one long braid, and her lips were bright red.

"Metchthild, we can't take you any farther," one of the soldiers told the dark-haired woman. "That applies to you, too," he said, motioning for Sara and Liese to get off. "We've taken you as far as we can."

No farther? Sara's head reeled, and she looked at Liese for support. "No!" Liese shouted and started to cry. "I won't get off!"

The soldier turned his head at Liese's outburst. "Take them with you," he said to the women.

"But what are we to do with them?" the blond woman asked.

"Take them to the Red Cross, Gudrun," the soldier replied. "They have children's homes, you know."

"We'll have enough trouble without two kids tagging along," Metchthild said bitterly.

Sara wanted to hide.

"Get going," the soldier said roughly. "We can't wait all day."

The women crawled off the truck and stood waiting. "You, too," the soldier said, glaring at Sara and Liese.

Sara hung her head, but Liese folded her arms in a determined gesture. "I'm not going unless they promise to take us to the children's home," she said.

"Stubborn girl!" the exasperated soldier said, shaking his head. He looked at the women. "You two promise to get these girls to an orphanage?"

"Oh, might as well," Metchthild said with a shrug of her shoulders. "Come on, let's get out of here."

CHAPTER 3

Sara slowly climbed off the truck. She wasn't sure she liked the women, but she didn't know what else to do. Metchthild walked away without even looking back, and Gudrun followed, motioning for the girls to do the same. They walked so fast that Sara had to run occasionally to keep up. Then without warning, the string that held up her right stocking snapped, and the sock slithered down her leg and bunched up at her ankle. The cold stung her bare legs, but she was afraid to pause long enough to fix it. Her stocking worked itself down around her shoe, and she began stepping on it. Now she *had* to stop.

"Come on," Liese called, "we have to keep going."

Sara pulled up her stocking with a jerk and ran to catch up, but before she had caught up with the others, it had fallen again. "My stocking!" she yelled. "It won't stay up."

"We can't stop," Liese said.

Sara was desperate. "Maybe if they knew we had food...." Her voice trailed off in the snowy air.

Liese ran and grabbed Gudrun's coat sleeves. "Stop!" she cried. "Sara's stocking is falling off." Gudrun turned and looked, then kept walking.

"Look, we have food!" Liese yelled.

Metchthild stopped. "You do?" she asked. "How much?"

"Three tins of fish and some butter," Liese said.

The women glanced at each other. "We could use that," Gudrun admitted. Then she really looked at the girls for the first time.

Liese stuck her hands in her pocket and pursed her lips in determination. Suddenly she started to cry. Sara knew she was only crying to get their attention.

"There, there," Gudrun said, patting Liese on the shoulder. "I guess we haven't been very nice. What's this about your stocking?" Liese pointed to Sara who pulled at her stocking and then let if fall. "Do we have anything to hold it up?" she asked Metchthild.

"Maybe I could divide the twine in my boots," Metchthild said. She took out one of her shoestrings, divided the twine into two strands, and gave one to Sara.

"Thank you," Sara said, pulling up her stocking. She pressed her legs together to hold it up, tied the string around her lower thigh, and folded the top edge of her stocking over the string.

"We'd better get going again," Metchthild said. "It will soon be dark, and the farther we get, the better."

This time the women walked beside them, slowing their pace to match that of the girls.

"We'd better start looking for a place to spend the night," Gudrun said as the sun started to set. "It won't be long before it's dark."

They found a barn, ate the frozen fish, and buried themselves in a pile of loose hay for the night. Sara was so tired she went to sleep the minute she closed her eyes. But in the middle of the night she was awakened by a persistent itching. Lice! She recognized them even in the dark. She crawled out of the makeshift bed, brushed herself off, and sat on top of the hay. The frosty air sent a shiver through her, and she realized she couldn't stay on top. She crawled back under the hay and closed her eyes.

"Wake up, wake up!" Someone was shaking her. Sara stretched slowly and tried to remember where she was. A faint light came in a small window, and she was aware of the dusty smell of hay.

"Come on, we have to get going," Gudrun said, shaking Sara again. "If we start now, perhaps we can get to the children's home before noon."

Sara pushed back the straw and awkwardly got to her feet. She itched all over, and her toes hurt. In spite of the fact that she felt like crying, she only twisted her face and picked the straw from her coat.

The sun gradually shed its light on the snowy landscape until it became a bright red ball at their backs. Sara followed the women mechanically, trying to ignore her painful toes and itching head.

Her hands were cold and she stuck them in her pocket. A hard lump lay in the bottom—the butter! Quickly, so no one else would notice, she stuck it in her mouth and sucked on it.

Suddenly Sara's wooden sole started to flap as the upper part tore away from the wooden base. "Oh, no," she groaned. "My shoe is broken."

The women stopped right away this time. "You really have a lot of problems," Metchthild said, but she didn't sound angry. She divided her other twine shoestring into two strands, and tied one around the end of Sara's shoe. "It'll probably wear through pretty soon," she said, "but maybe it will hold until we get to the children's home. It shouldn't be too much longer."

It worked well enough so that Sara could walk, but snow came through the crack in her boot and her sock was soon wet. Her toes hurt more than ever, and she started to limp. Now all her energies were used in forcing that one foot forward.

Gudrun picked a louse off Sara's coat. "If you don't walk faster, the little fellows will catch up with you and crawl up the back of your leg," she teased. Sara laughed in spite of herself and felt better.

It wasn't long until Metchthild pointed to a large stone house in the distance. "There it is," she said. Sara straightened, wiped her dripping nose with the back of her hand, and walked faster.

A stone walkway led to the heavy wooden door. Sara stood still, her stiffened arms pushed deep into the pockets of her short coat, as Gudrun knocked. The knocks resounded with a hollow sound that sent a shiver up Sara's tense arms. Gudrun waited and knocked again, but there was no answer.

"Go around the back," Gudrun said. "Maybe you can find someone there."

Metchthild disappeared around the corner, and Gudrun continued rapping. "There has to be someone here," she said in a determined voice.

Sara bit her lip and kicked at the snow. What was taking them so long? "Anybody home?" Gudrun called, but the door threw back the question with a mocking echo.

Metchthild came running from behind the house. "They all left several hours ago," she said. "A neighbor told me. He said they decided to move the children farther west for safety. They were going by train, so perhaps if we go to the station they'll still be there. Hurry, it's this way."

Sara forgot about her aching toes and ran as fast as she could. They had to go to the station before the children left! Her shoe started to flop again, but still she ran. Then the sole folded back underneath her foot and she tripped, falling flat on the snowy street. She picked herself up only to see the others still running. Quickly she untied her boot, took it off, and ran with only her stocking on. The damp toe of her sock soon froze solid, and gradually the wet snow penetrated the heavy wool all along the bottom of her foot.

With sudden fear, Sara realized that she couldn't see the others. "Oh no," she cried. "Where did they go?" She stopped, looking around in confusion.

Gudrun appeared from around a street corner, waving her arms. "We found the station," she yelled, "and they haven't left yet. . . . What happened to your shoe?" she asked as Sara ran toward her.

"The string broke, so I took it off."

"For heaven's sakes, your foot will be frozen. Get in here quick and take off those wet socks." Sara followed her inside the railroad station. Small babies, crying toddlers, tall girls—a crowd of children filled the room. Sara sat down next to Liese while Gudrun left to find the person in charge.

Sara's foot began to throb as she pulled off her stiff stocking. Her toes were a grayish white, and on the bottom of her big toe was a watery blister. The rest of her foot was a reddish purple. She took off her scarf and wrapped it firmly around her aching limb.

When Sara straightened and looked around, Gudrun was returning with a woman in a long black dress and white pinafore. "This is Sister Katrina," she explained, introducing the woman whose friendly face was framed in a white scarf that tied behind her neck. "She will be taking care of you."

"I hear you have a cold foot," Sister Katrina said. "Do you mind if I look at it?" Sara unwrapped her foot, and Sister Katrina knelt to examine it. "Let me see if I can find something warm to wrap it in."

"We have to get moving," Metchthild said when Sister Katrina had left. "You girls should be well taken care of now." She gave them each a pat on the head.

"Thank you," Sara said, but Metchthild was already out the

door. Gudrun smiled at them and quickly followed.

Sister Katrina returned with a dry wool sock. "This should warm you up," she said. "Your foot will probably start itching when it gets warm, but try not to break the blister with scratching. You can wrap your scarf around it again for more warmth if you want. Just try not to get your sock wet on your way to the train. Hop or something." She smiled, and Sara relaxed a little.

"Where are we going?" Liese asked.

"To an old castle in southern Germany. By the way, do you girls think you could help with some of the smaller children? I'll give you a baby that you can hold on your lap so you don't need to walk," she said, looking at Sara. "Liese, you come with me."

Sister Katrina returned with a baby named Greta. She sat quietly on Sara's lap, nibbling a piece of bread and leaning her head heavily on Sara's chest. She had slobbered the front of her sweater wet, and the bread had disintegrated into a soupy mess that dribbled down her arms and all over Sara's coat. Sara was thankful that Greta was so contented. Across the room, Liese was trying to comfort a small boy who whined constantly and pulled at his ear. A baby was crying, and the little ones had become fretful.

It seemed to Sara that the train would never come. The group of children became a blur in front of her tired eyes. Her thigh became numb, and the bottom of her right foot stung with a prickly sensation. Greta grew heavier by the minute and rolled her eyes in an effort to keep awake.

At last Sara heard the rumble of an approaching locomotive and the loud swishing of brakes. The children ran to the window in excitement. Their train had finally come! Sara picked up Greta, limped through the snow to the train, and dropped into the nearest seat.

The train blew its whistle and slowly began to move. Suddenly there was a different sound—a wailing scream that sent a shiver down Sara's spine. "Air raid, air raid—that's the siren!" a boy shouted. A flash of bright light forced Sara to close her eyes for a second. She placed Greta on the seat and stood up to look out the window. The whole sky seemed to be on fire—a giant torch that licked hungrily at the darkened city, devouring everything within its terrible grasp.

Below her, Sara could feel the clicking of the wheels picking up speed. She grabbed the back of the seat to brace herself against the sway of the accelerating train. Faster and faster the train carried them out of town and beyond the intense heat and light. Sara pressed her face to the window as the light seared the picture into her mind. She *had* to watch—to make sure that they were moving away from it and that the terrible horror was not overtaking them.

CHAPTER 4

Sara was awakened by the sound of chimes. She looked around in confusion. Then she remembered—the train had left the station just in time. She shuddered, trying to shake off the memory of the blazing city. The train ride had been long, but now she was safe inside a large, sturdy castle. The long room in which she lay was lined with beds.

From where she was, Sara could look out the window and see the clock. It was the first thing she had noticed about the castle. Built into a tall tower, it was like a faithful watchman chiming every fifteen minutes, and striking out the hours with drumlike precision. The castle itself was built of gray stone. Its heavy door could be locked from the inside with a huge crossbar that banged when it was dropped. Last night after her hair had been thoroughly washed and treated for lice, Sara had stood near the door when darkness came, just to watch it being fastened. Looking at the massive beam which she was sure even the Russians couldn't break, she had felt safe.

Sara propped herself on her elbow and stared at nothing in particular. Now that she had time to think, she wondered where Mama and Papa were. Her memory returned to the pine tree, and she tried to understand. Why had they left her? Her lip quivered, and she grabbed the pillow. Maybe they didn't love her after all. Maybe they just wanted to get rid of her. Maybe they had left on purpose. The "maybe's" grew bigger and bigger until her lip stopped quivering and stuck out in an angry scowl. Well, if they didn't love her anymore, she wouldn't love them either! She drew the pillow close and hit it with her fist. Then she fell into it and cried. Maybe they were hurt. Maybe the Russians had captured them and sent them to Siberia.

The clock struck seven times. Sara counted the chimes and sat up. "I really don't know what happened," she told herself with a sigh. The beds on either side were empty, and she could hear voices down the hall in the bathroom.

"Oooh," she moaned as she put her weight on her frozen toes. She shifted her weight to the other foot, put on her slip, and hobbled down the hall.

The bathroom was crowded with girls. The boys were on the third floor and the babies in the nursery down below. Sara took her place in line and smiled shyly at the girl in front of her. Her frozen toes itched unbearably, and she rubbed her other foot over them in an attempt to scratch them.

The chimes marked the quarter hour as Sara quickly washed her face. She limped down to her room and hurriedly dressed. Liese was waiting for her to go to breakfast.

In the dining hall were long tables with benches on either side. "How many children do you think there are?" Sara asked, looking around the crowded room.

"There are seven tables," Liese counted.

Sara looked up and down her bench. There were fourteen girls sitting at her table. "What's fourteen times seven?" she asked.

The girl across from her drew the problem on the table with her finger. "Ninety-eight," she concluded. "With the babies there would be over a hundred."

For breakfast there was rye bread and milk. Sara hungrily took a bite and then paused and looked at Liese. "No salt," Liese said, licking her lips in disappointment. Sara sighed and took another bite. It was about as tasty as sawdust, but it still felt good in her empty stomach.

After breakfast, Sister Katrina explained to them the rules for living together. "Each of you will make your own bed and take turns doing the dishes and cleaning. Afternoons will be spent doing schoolwork, and there will be free time in the evenings. But you *must* drop everything and go to the basement immediately every time the air raid siren blows." Sara shivered, and several of the children stood up with a jolt as if the siren had actually sounded.

"How do we get to the basement?" one of the girls asked in a strained voice.

"You can line up by the door," Sister Katrina explained, "and

I'll take you there. Then you can explore the grounds around the castle. But at ten o'clock I want all the girls back here so we can fit you with some clothes."

Benches scraped the floor and dishes clattered as the children picked up their plates and took them to the kitchen. Sara waited until everyone was off the bench and then swung her legs over it and limped after them.

The basement shelter was damp and dimly lit. After her eyes had adjusted, Sara could see gray stone walls and thick beams overhead. But she was confused. "Are they dropping bombs here, too?" she asked Liese. "We're in Germany, aren't we? Papa told me we'd be safe from the Russians in Germany."

A boy from behind them answered. "You girls don't know anything about this war. The Russians are fighting us in the east, but the Americans and British are fighting us in the west. They won't win, though. Germany is the greatest! Heil Hitler!" He saluted and clicked his heels. "I'd fight if I were old enough!" he bragged, then turned and marched away with a brisk goose step.

Sara stared after him. Why would anyone want to go to war? She had heard Papa talk about how Mennonites didn't believe in fighting. Many years ago they had arranged with the Russian government to take care of the forests instead of going to the army. But that was before the Communists had come. She scanned the sky for airplanes. Was Germany strong enough to fight off enemies on both sides at once? She walked slowly into the castle and lay on her bed. At least the castle seemed safe. She stared out at the clock tower without really seeing it. Her foot throbbed, and her throat was tight.

The clock struck the hour. Sara absently counted each gong and then sat up quickly. Ten o'clock! She hopped down the steps one at a time and followed the voices coming from a room beyond the dining area. She opened the door and then stopped. Never in her life had she seen so many clothes! There was a whole row of dresses—short ones at the front of the room, gradually getting longer and longer toward the back.

Sara walked down the row until the dresses looked about her size, then she pushed them apart one at a time to see if there were any pretty ones. Suddenly she stopped, and her mouth dropped open. There was a pink dress with ruffles down the

front. Sara reached out and caught the hem of the dress in her right hand and stroked the smooth, sheer fabric with the left. Her heart pounded as she took it off the rack and gently held it against her. It looked like a perfect fit! Quickly she picked out several more dresses and went to have Sister Katrina check them out. But all the time her mind was on the pink one.

"This isn't a dress you can wear every day," Sister Katrina said when she saw it. "Are you sure you want this one?"

Sara's toes throbbed, and her hands were wet. "Yes," she said, and gulped hard.

Sister Katrina looked at her closely and then back at the dress. "It is beautiful," she said, "but where are you going to wear it?"

Sara's face was hot and she felt like crying. "To church," she finally said, even though she didn't know if there was a church.

"You may keep it, then," Sister Katrina said.

Sara beamed and said, "Thank you" so fast that Sister Katrina smiled.

A strange lady was sitting behind the desk with Sister Katrina. On her gray uniform she wore a patch displaying the black bent cross of the Nazis—the swastika. She handed Sara a neck scarf and a red badge with the same black emblem. "Wear them for Germany," she said.

Sara carefully put the scarf and the badge on top of her pink dress and carried them up to her bed. "If Germany won, would the war stop?" she wondered. It was her only hope. She tied the scarf around her neck and pinned the badge on her collar. Then she picked up the pink dress, held it against her, and imagined how it would be to actually wear it.

Five weeks passed and Sara had not worn her dress. But tomorrow was Easter and she would wear it to church for the first time. Sara laid the dress out carefully, then picked up her towel and ran to the bathroom. She wanted to tell Liese the news. "Did you see those eggs in the kitchen?" she asked as she joined Liese in line for a bath. "A whole basket full! I think Sister Katrina is going to hide them for Easter."

"Oh, good," Liese said, clapping her hands.

"Shh," Sara whispered, pulling at Liese's arm. "I'm not sure that's what they're for."

"I'll ask Sister Katrina," Liese said. "She'll tell me."

Sara felt her ears grow hot. "Oh, no, don't tell her I saw them."

"Why? I'm not scared."

"I don't want you to, that's all," Sara replied lamely. It wasn't the first time she had felt embarrassed by Liese's boldness.

"I'll just ask if we're going to have a hunt," Liese said.

"Next," a voice called out from behind the blanket partition.

Sara entered the enclosure, undressed, and stepped into the big round tub. Brrr—the water wasn't very warm anymore. She quickly rubbed the water over her body with her hands, stepped out of the tub, and wrapped herself in a towel. Liese peeked around the blanket. "Hey," she whispered. "I asked Sister Katrina, and she said that she's going to hide the eggs so we can hunt them in the morning."

"Yea!" Sara said, running back to her bed. She pulled on her white nightgown and danced around her bed. She could hardly wait until tomorrow.

CHAPTER 5

Morning arrived with an airy lightness. Sara stretched beneath her covers and then settled back to watch the sunbeams that sparkled on a trail of dust from the window to the foot of her bed. Easter! She sat up, put her feet on the cool floor, and went to the window. A cherry tree was white with clusters of tiny blossoms, and the stems of a forsythia bush were covered with hundreds of golden flowers. Somewhere, a skylark trilled a cascade of clear, high notes.

"Sara," someone whispered right beside her.

Sara jumped, then laughed when she recognized Liese. "I didn't know you were up," she said.

"I want to ask Sister Katrina if we can get the eggs before breakfast," Liese said. She hurried to find her, but stopped short at the doorway.

"Happy Easter!" Sister Katrina greeted her. "What are you doing up so early?"

"May we get the eggs now?" Liese asked.

Sister Katrina wrinkled up her forehead. "All right," she said after a pause. "Why don't you wake up the rest of the girls? We can eat breakfast later."

"Oh, good," Liese said. She cupped her hands around her mouth and shouted, "Get up, everybody. We can get our eggs before breakfast."

The grass felt wet on Sara's bare feet, and the spring air sent a chill through her white nightgown. She walked toward the forsythia bush, drawn by the strong sweetness of the flowers.

Suddenly the scream of an air raid siren shattered the morning stillness. "Quick, everybody into the shelter!" Sister Katrina commanded.

Sara pulled up the skirt of her nightgown and ran for the basement steps. In the dim light she could see it was already crowded. She plopped down on the hard floor and pulled her knees up to her chin. "How could anyone ruin such a beautiful day?" she wondered, tears stinging her eyes. She wiped them on the sleeve of her nightgown and stared into the corner.

What was this war about, anyway? She remembered her cousin Karl in his new gray uniform, just after he had been drafted into the German army. On his shiny belt buckle was the inscription *Gott mit uns*—God with us. She had felt sure Germany was good. Now American planes were destroying Germany. Could God be with the Americans, too? That would mean that God was fighting against himself. Why would he do that? She hugged her knees tighter, feeling the hardness of her knobby knees on her cheek. If God was God, he couldn't be that dumb. She sighed heavily. War didn't make sense.

Half an hour later the all-clear siren told them it was safe. "Let's go up and have some breakfast," Sister Katrina said. Sara straightened her stiff legs, walked out into the smoke-filled air, and squinted against the clouded sun. The castle was still standing! In front of it, the forsythia splashed a dash of yellow, and the skylark sang from its nest in the budding cherry tree. Perhaps it could be a good day after all.

"If you hurry, I think there will still be time to get ready for the Easter service," Sister Katrina said to the older children after breakfast.

"What about the eggs?" Liese asked.

"We can get them later," Sara suggested.

"As soon as we get back," Liese decided.

Sara hurried to get ready. She fingered the ruffle on her pink dress and ran her fingers over the smooth softness of the sheer fabric.

"You look beautiful," Liese said when Sara had finished dressing.

Sara blushed. Once Marga had told her the same thing, but that was long ago back in Russia. "You look pretty, too," she said shyly.

From the front of the castle, Sara could see the steeple of the church down in the valley. The children walked across the lawn and into the cool freshness of the wooded hillside. The sun filtered through the budding branches, and here and there clumps of narcissus grew wild. Sara reached down and picked one. In the center of its circle of delicate petals a graceful trumpet raised its pale yellow bell. Just what she needed, she decided, and stuck it in her hair.

Above her, Sara heard the whir of airplanes followed by the shriek of the siren. "Hang onto a tree!" Sister Katrina shouted.

Sara grabbed the nearest trunk and squeezed tightly against it. The bark felt rough against her face and snagged at her dress. Above her a motor slowed and then raced. Beneath her, the earth trembled and the whole world seemed to explode.

"The Home, the Home!" someone shouted. "They hit the Home!"

Red hot anger surged up inside Sara—an anger stronger than fear. She turned to look and saw that the clock tower lay crumbled in a pile of broken rubble.

Again she heard the surging power of an accelerating engine and looked up to see another plane dive toward its target. On its side a white star surrounded by a blue circle told her it belonged to the Americans. There was a flash of light followed by a thundering roar. Sara could feel the tree tremble at its roots and smell the heavy dust of explosives.

Just as suddenly, it was quiet. "Come," Sister Katrina said in a low voice. "Let's go home."

Sara walked slowly. Smoke hung so thick in the air that it seemed to Sara that the flowers drooped and the trees bowed their heads. Even the skylark was silent.

She stepped over a pile of stones and looked up at the jagged wall of the children's home. Where was the clock? Her eyes scanned the rubble until she saw a narrow piece of iron imbedded in the heap of stone. One of the clock's hands! She pulled at it, but it didn't budge.

Several older boys returned from a run around the building. "They only got this corner," one of them said.

"Any broken windows?" Sister Katrina asked.

"One in the kitchen."

Sara couldn't even feel happy that the rest of the building was untouched. She stood frozen, staring at the ugly gash in the wall of the castle.

Sister Katrina put her arm around Sara's shoulder. Then she

reached up and gently pulled the flower from Sara's hair. "It's beautiful," she said. "Even in all this trouble there is something beautiful." She handed it back to Sara and murmured, "I guess that's what Easter is all about."

Sara looked down at the ruffled edge at the top of the flower. "It's beautiful," she repeated, then went inside and put it under her pillow.

Liese came dashing in. "What's that for?" she wanted to know.

"Oh, nothing," Sara said, her cheeks turning hot.

"Let's go see if we can find the eggs."

The siren sounded before they even got out the door.

"I'm not going to the shelter," Liese said, grabbing Sara and scanning the sky. "They *can't* hit the Home again."

A squadron of planes flew overhead, huddled together like a flock of geese. One left the group, accelerated into a nose dive, then climbed to join its comrades. Beyond the trees Sara could see the church steeple shoot up and then fall. There was an ear-splitting crash and a cloud of white smoke enveloped the building, cutting off the view.

"Sara! Liese!" Sister Katrina grabbed them by the arms and pulled them into the cellar. "What do you think you're doing?"

"We don't want them to hit the castle again," Sara murmured.

"Watching won't keep the bombs from falling." Sister Katrina was firm. "Don't you ever do that again. Buildings can be rebuilt; people can't. You understand?"

Sara lowered her head and huddled on the damp floor, listening for the airplanes. But all she could hear was the tense breathing of fearful children. By the time the all-clear siren finally blew, her stomach was growling, announcing that it was far past lunchtime."

"It's safe," Sister Katrina said. "Let's go see if we can get some lunch."

Sara ate, but the food stuck in her throat. As soon as she could, she went to the bedroom and lifted her pillow. The flower was there—withered and flattened, but still beautiful.

"Sara!" Liese called. "Where are you?"

Sara quickly put the flower back under her pillow. "Here," she called.

"Come on, let's see if we can get the eggs. . . ."

The siren screamed its warning right on cue. Too tired and

discouraged to feel anything, Sara shuffled into the basement. Leaning her head against the rough wall, she tried to sleep.

"Wake up," Liese nudged her several hours later. "We can go out now. They're gone."

Slowly Sara stood up and stretched her cramped legs. Outside, the sun sat like a fiery ball on the horizon, its light falling in a colorful display on the surrounding sky.

"Come on, let's get the eggs," Liese said for the fourth time.

The cherry tree was snowy white against the blazing sun, and the skylark sang somewhere among its branches. A slight breeze brought the smell of forsythia. Sara walked toward the smell and spread the stiff stems. There, camouflaged among the bright flowers, was a yellow egg.

"Got one!" she shouted.

Although the bombing continued through the next month, it never was so heavy again. Then on May 7, 1945, Sister Katrina announced that the war was over. Sara's eyes widened, and she straightened to attention as she joined the others in cheering the good news. Several boys whistled. The little ones danced around, not quite understanding, but wanting to be a part of the excitement.

"Who won?" Liese asked.

"The Allies," Sister Katrina replied.

"Not the Germans?" Liese asked in disbelief.

Sara stopped clapping, and her heart fell. She had been counting on Germany to win. Did that mean that the Russians would come?

Liese grabbed her hand. "Come on," she said, holding her Nazi badge and neck scarf in her other hand. "Let's get rid of these. If the Americans find out we were for Germany, we'll be in trouble." They went out to the garden, dug a hole, and buried the telltale emblems.

As they walked back to the castle, an airplane flew overhead. "To the shelter!" Sara screamed and ran to the basement steps. Liese followed, as did a group of little children who were playing ring-around-the-rosy. They sat huddled in fear as they had so many times before.

"Children, children!" Sister Katrina said, coming down the steps. "The war is over. You don't need to be afraid of the airplanes now. They won't drop bombs anymore."

Sara relaxed somewhat and managed an embarrassed smile. But there was something she still wanted to know. "Can the Russians get us now?" she asked the Sister anxiously.

"No, dear," said Sister Katrina quietly, putting her arm around Sara's shoulder. "No one can get you now." They climbed out of the dark cellar and into the warm sunshine.

It seemed to Sara that a great heaviness was lifting now that the days were uninterrupted by the screaming siren. Tonight, it felt especially good to be eating a warm supper surrounded by so many friends. She finished her meal and sat back on her chair for the evening prayers and announcements. But she wasn't prepared for what Sister Katrina had to say. "Our food supplies are very low. We've decided it would be better for you to live on farms where there is more food."

"You mean we can't stay here anymore?" Liese asked.

"That's right. You'll live with a farm family."

Sara's breath came in short gasps, and her hands moistened with sweat. How could Sister Katrina do such a thing? *This* was her home.

"We don't mind being hungry," said Gretchen, one of the bigger girls.

"We want to stay," said another.

"No!" The word resounded again and again as the children grasped what was happening.

"I'm staying with you," Sara whispered to Liese. She put her arm through Liese's and held it tight. But when they approached Sister Katrina about it, she looked at them sadly and explained that few homes could take more than one child.

Sara's throat ached. She ran to the bedroom, flopped herself on her bed, and cried until she was too tired to cry anymore.

Then she rolled onto her side and stared at the wall. Was there any place in the whole world for her? First Mama and Papa had left her, and now she couldn't even stay here. She pulled her pillow angrily toward her and a pressed narcissus fell on the floor. Something beautiful. . . . Well, maybe there was for someone, but not for her. Leaving the flower where it fell, she buried her head and tried to sleep.

CHAPTER 6

"Sara!" Sara rolled over and then sat up quickly. It was dark, so she must have slept. "Sara, it's me," Liese said, sitting down on Sara's bed. "What are we going to do?"

"I don't know," Sara whispered, "but I don't want to go to any old farm."

"Me, either," Liese said. "I'm not going." They sat in stubborn silence.

"I'm not going to do the dishes tomorrow," Liese said.

"Or make my bed," Sara added.

"Let's none of us do anything."

They woke the other girls and explained their plan. "And if we get into trouble, it's just too bad!" said Gretchen, quickly agreeing to their plan. The other girls also agreed. Finally they all returned to their beds.

"Stay here to sleep," Sara said. Liese crawled in beside her and curled up in a ball. Sara lay as stiff as the hard bed beneath her. She could hear Liese's breathing become more heavy and regular, but her own eyes remained as wide as those of the night owl she heard hooting in the nearby woods. Papa and Mama were very much on her mind. Her chest felt heavy and her throat was tight. She scooted closer to Liese and buried her head in the pillow.

On her way to breakfast, Sara paused and looked around. On her bed lay a pile of disheveled covers, a pillow propped awkwardly against the headboard, and a rumpled nightgown. Nineteen other beds were similarly disarrayed. They had to be made before they could eat—that was the rule.

Sara went into the dining room, sat down at the table, and hung her head. Out of the corner of her eyes, she could see Sister

Katrina coming from the bedroom. "Girls, you must make your beds before you can have breakfast," she said firmly. Sara looked at the bony ridges of her knuckles. No one moved.

Sister Katrina nervously tapped her foot and fastened her tired, gray eyes on the girls. A hot flush crawled slowly up Sara's neck and settled on her cheeks. "All right, then, go to your bedroom immediately," Sister Katrina said, looking rather sad. Sara quickly stood up, stumbled over the long bench, and went to the bedroom. She flung herself down on the rumpled bed and lay perfectly still. Up and down the room she could hear harsh whispers and muffled sobs. Her bottom lip stuck out in a determined scowl and then trembled. She shut her eyes tight to hold back the gathering tears, but one squeezed out and trickled down her cheek.

After a long while Sister Katrina reappeared. "The little children have finished eating," she said. "You must make your beds and do the breakfast dishes before ten o'clock. I expect you to cooperate."

Sara buried her head in her pillow. She didn't want to be bad—she just wanted to stay. Now that she had finally found a place, she was not going to have it taken away.

At ten o'clock when Sister Katrina returned, nothing had been done. She stood quietly, looking wearily at the dejected girls. "What are we going to do?" she said finally.

"Let us stay," Liese said boldly.

"There isn't enough food."

"I'd rather be hungry and stay here," Gretchen said, nervously twisting her braid.

"I lived on one of those farms before I came here," a stocky girl named Hildur added bitterly, "and all they wanted was my work."

"You may have to work," Sister Katrina admitted, "but I don't think you will have to do more than you can. The farmers are the only ones who have food."

"Can't we grow our own food?" one of the boys asked.

"There are too many of us," Sister Katrina said, shaking her head.

"We could all help," Hildur protested. "I would work hard if we could stay here."

The smaller girls had started to cry, and the older ones sat rigid and motionless.

"I'm not sure we can grow enough food even then. Besides, it will be a few months before we can harvest anything we plant," Sister Katrina said slowly.

Sara breathed heavily, and her hands were cold and white. "We will eat less," she said in a shaky voice. "We just want to stay here."

"Yes, . . ." the girls shook their heads in agreement.

"Why is it so important to stay here?" Sister Katrina asked softly.

"Our friends are here," Liese said.

"This is our home," Sara added.

Sister Katrina looked around the room. "I have no choice," she said firmly. "You must have food."

Sara's heart fluttered and her arms felt weak. The room swam in front of her eyes. She flopped herself down on the bed and sobbed until her pillow was wet.

There was no lunch, and in the afternoon school session the students were silent and sullen. By evening, Sister Katrina had decided to serve supper, but much of the food remained untouched. Sara slept fitfully, and she could tell from the sobs scattered throughout the room that others were also awake.

The next morning Sara sat on the edge of her bed and methodically stroked the sheets smooth. She was too tired to make her bed and too discouraged not to. She heard the quick steps and soft swish of the long black dress as Sister Katrina came into the room. Sara didn't look up, but she could see that the Sister had stopped and was silently looking around at the despondent girls.

"I will be gone all day," she started quietly. "You girls will need to manage things alone." She cleared her throat and put her hands under the apron of her white pinafore. "I know you want to stay, so I'm going to see if I can gather up any food for us. I can't promise, but I will try."

The girls erupted with a burst of noise and descended on Sister Katrina. She held out her arms to the girls, and tears rolled down her cheeks. "Remember, I can't promise," she repeated.

"That's all right, that's all right. You don't need to promise—just *do* it!" one of the small girls shouted as she jumped up and down.

Sister Katrina chuckled and put her hand on the child's head. "I'll do my best," she said. "Now get to work. We have a lot to do today. Good-bye."

"Good-bye!" the girls shouted and scurried to their individual tasks. Within a few minutes the beds looked as if no one had ever slept in them. In fact, all day they worked as if their lives depended on it. Sister Katrina had to let them stay—she just *had* to.

There was a mood of tense expectancy at supper. Sister Katrina returned midway through the meal and walked quickly into the kitchen. Sara kept looking up from her plate to watch the doorway. She shoved part of the food to the side of her plate and tried to imagine what it would be like to only have half as much. Her mouth watered and her stomach felt hollow, but she was sure she could manage if only she could stay at the Home. Having convinced herself that she could do it, she picked up her fork and ate the rest.

When they had finished eating, Sister Katrina entered the room, stood quietly, and folded her hands like she did when she was ready to make an announcement. One hundred pairs of eyes looked intently at her. Her mouth was set in a straight line, and her eyes looked tired.

"She must have not found enough food," Sara thought. She shifted nervously on the bench and held onto it tightly.

"I realize that being together is very important to you children—more important than always having a full plate." Sara nodded and squeezed the bench until her hands hurt. "I have managed to get enough food to last us until we can get food from the garden. We will have to work hard, and there may not always be enough to eat. But I think you are very wise children—you have learned the true meaning of courage. We can face a lot of things as long as we love each other. You may stay."

Sara's eyes widened, and her mouth dropped open. She clapped her hands and shouted. The room echoed with the voices of one hundred jubilant children. They would stay together!

The children worked hard turning up the ground for their garden. They picked up stones from the rocky soil and worked it smooth with tools made from steel pieces pulled out of the castle rubble. But they could do nothing with the ugly black bomb

crater. It lay in the middle of the garden like an open wound,
filling with rain water that turned murky with staleness and then
disappeared.

 As the weeks passed, rows of tiny green plants peeked out of
the black soil, and the children were no longer allowed to walk
freely on the garden. They walked along the edges, watching the
tiny plants grow and quickly uprooting any strange weed that
might appear. Soon it was easy to distinguish the rows of
cabbages, turnips, and potatoes. The children relaxed and felt
certain that there would be food.

One early summer day Sara and Liese were in the garden cutting spinach for lunch. They worked slowly, not so much because they disliked the job of cutting the crinkly, dark green leaves, but because they didn't like the thought of it sitting in stringy piles on their plates.

"Sister Katrina says it's good for us," Liese groaned.

"I'll just hold my nose," Sara said, and stood up to practice.

"Liese! Liese!" Sister Katrina called.

"We'd better hurry," Liese said. Sara let go of her nose and started cutting spinach.

"Liese!" Sister Katrina called again as she appeared around the corner of the castle. "Oh, there you are," she said. "I've been looking for you. Someone's here to see you."

"Me?" Liese asked. "Come on, Sara, let's go see who it is." She ran to the castle with Sara trailing at her heels.

CHAPTER 7

"Mama!" Liese cried. She was already in her mother's arms. There they stood laughing and crying all at the same time. Sara looked at the floor.

"Oh, Liese! I'm so glad you're here. I didn't know what had happened to you."

"We tried to find you, but you were gone," Liese said all in one breath.

"The soldiers needed the road, so they forced us onto another route. We waited as long as we could. Franz borrowed a bicycle and went all over looking for you and Sara. Finally they said we had to go—the Russians were so close. . . ." Frau Rempel hugged Liese again, and tears streamed down her face.

So they *had* tried to find them. A lump formed in Sara's throat.

"How did you know I was here?" Liese asked.

"Through the Red Cross. I went to their office every day to see if they had any information about you."

A tear slowly trickled down Sara's cheek. Suddenly Frau Rempel noticed her. She put her arm around her and gave her a quick squeeze. "I think I know where your parents are. I'll try to get word to them that you're here. They are so worried."

Sara stared at Frau Rempel until her image became blurry. Then she ran up the steps to her bed. Her mind was crowded with images from the past. She was returning to the tree and no one was there. For the first time she imagined the wagon disappearing down the road. Her mother was crying, and her father was biting his lip. Maybe they had really cared. Would they come all the way to Ansbach to get her? What if Frau Rempel couldn't contact them? Her sobs came from deep within and her body shook. When she finally stopped crying, her body grew limp, and she felt tired. She closed her eyes and slept.

The following day Sara stood at the castle door as Liese and her mother walked away down the cobblestone path. In her mind she was running after Liese, pulling her back. The next minute she was Liese, and the woman at her side was her own mother. What would it feel like? She tried to remember her mother—she was in the kitchen back in Russia, pushing straw into the large brick oven, then punching and pulling the dark rye dough until it was smooth and stretchy. Her hands moved quickly, filling the baking pans with small, rounded loaves. Would she come?

Sara turned to Liese, but Liese was gone. Setting her mouth in a determined line, she walked with wooden steps around the castle. A pile of stones stood like a blockade, separating her from the courtyard at the back. She looked up at the clock tower standing naked and exposed except for one cracked and shifted wall. She knew how it felt. She sat down and cried for the building because she would not cry for herself.

Summer dragged by—hot, sticky days when the pocked countryside tried to yield food for the hungry, discouraged people. The children were harvesting potatoes, turnips, and cabbages from their garden, but the huge crater lay like an ugly wound in the middle of it and yielded nothing.

Sara missed Liese. Although she had embarrassed Sara occasionally, Liese's outgoing nature had helped Sara overcome some of her shyness.

Now that Liese was gone, Sara found herself longing for Marga—not the efficient and responsible Marga, but the Marga who, like Sara, was very sensitive and sometimes fearful. Marga understood her so well. She could have told Marga about the flower, for instance, but Liese wouldn't have understood. Still, she wished Liese were around to make things happen.

Fall came, and across the hillsides the vineyards were heavy with grapes. Still no one had come. Morning after morning Sara woke up with an expectant ache, only to go to bed with it still there.

Then one day a visitor was announced for Sara. She stood, frozen to one spot while hope and fear fought within her. Was it her family? But what if it wasn't? Would she know them if they came?

Forcing herself to walk slowly, she went into the dining room. Marga! She ran across the room and threw herself into Marga's arms. Laughing and crying, she hugged Marga, then laughed some more.

"Where's Mama?" she asked when she could finally talk.

"She had to stay with Papa," Marga said. "He's not well."

A heaviness gripped Sara. Why was Papa always sick?

"The worst part is that Franz is in jail," Marga went on. "We came together, but only one of us had a traveling pass. I was afraid that would happen, but Mama said we both had to come. Franz has to stay in jail for ten days, plus pay a fine. So we'll have to wait until he can get out before we go home."

Home. "Where's that?" Sara wanted to know.

"Hattorf. We live in an upstairs room. I don't know how long we can stay there because it's right on the border of the Russian Zone. But Papa couldn't go any farther."

Oh well, that didn't matter as long as Marga had come. Sara grabbed Marga and pulled her along to her room.

That night Marga slept in Liese's old bed. "Marga," Sara said, propping herself up on one arm, "you still there?"

"Yes."

"How did you know I was here?"

"Frau Rempel sent us a letter—she knew we had stopped at Hattorf. I guess she figured we were still there."

They tried to sleep. Sara propped herself up again. "Marga, are we going to walk to Hattorf?"

"We'll go by train after we get Franz out of jail."

Sara was wide awake. "Marga," she whispered again, "I'm so happy I can't sleep."

"Me, too," Marga said. "Tell me how you got here."

"Oh, we just walked," Sara said. "Marga, are you still there?"

Marga laughed and Sara joined in. It was good to be together again.

Ten days went by quickly, and before she knew it, Sara was saying good-bye to Sister Katrina and her friends in the children's home. Walking with Marga on the road to Nuremburg, she looked back at the castle, but it had become just another clump of rocks jutting out of the evergreen forest. Suddenly it seemed very far away. Hattorf and Papa and Mama seemed even farther. An unexpected heaviness weighed Sara down. What kind of house did they live in? Would they still remember her? Where would she sleep tonight? Her head began to spin as a hundred questions demanded answers. Her pace slowed to a dragging walk. With a start she realized that Marga was several meters ahead of her, and she ran to catch up—she was not going to let Marga out of her sight again.

It seemed to Sara that the whole world lay in ruins. The landscape was an endless series of solitary walls standing ragged and windowless among piles of broken bricks. And yet there were people—people as broken as the buildings from which they came. Villagers stood motionless in long lines, waiting for food. Women pushed carts full of straggly sticks. Men rode bicycles without tires, somehow made usable with rope tied around the rims. People picked up and stacked bricks out of the infinite pile of rubble. Was this what it would be like in Hattorf? A nagging fear sat like a rock in the pit of her stomach.

It was nearing supper time, and Sara was tired and hungry. The sky was clouding over, and the cool October air gradually crept through her coat. They entered a small village, picking their way through the littered streets. When they saw a sign that said WARMING ROOM, Marga stopped. "I wonder what a warming room is. Let's go in and see." She opened the door uncertainly.

"Come in," a woman greeted them.

"Thank you," Marga murmured.

"You traveling?" the woman asked, looking at the rucksacks on their backs.

"Yes, walking to Nuremburg," Marga answered.

"Then you'll probably want to stay here for the night. Find a cot, and I'll bring you something to eat." Marga looked as relieved as Sara felt.

The woman brought them a bowl of hot soup, and Sara drank it hungrily. It sent a warmth all the way through her. Her eyes drooped and her legs ached. She put the bowl on the floor beside her cot, lay down, and pulled the covers up to her chin. Her eyes slowly blinked and then stayed shut. She felt heavy on the sagging cot, and the thick blanket made her warm and very sleepy. She opened her eyes for a moment to make sure Marga was still there, and then slept soundly.

The next afternoon they reached Nuremburg. Its walls stood thick and strong, one of the few things for miles around that the war had not destroyed. They followed a well-worn path through the rubble to an entrance in the wall and entered the city. There it was—a junkyard of what must have once been a beautiful city. Twin steeples, burned black, guarded a pile of bricks that once was a church. Here and there a standing wall outlined the corner of a building which now lay in a heap. Steel frames, as useless as skinned umbrellas, stuck out of the mounds of brick and board. Sara stood staring in frozen silence. How could anyone do such a thing? As far as she could see, only a few buildings stood whole. Her body tightened with anger.

"Come on," Marga said, pulling at her impatiently. "We have

to get Franz."

They followed the detours around blocked streets until they reached a small entrance leading underneath a mass of junk. It was the police station. "We've come for Franz Friesen," Marga told the officer.

He grunted and paged through a book. "For traveling without a pass—ten days and one hundred marks," he read. "The ten days are up. What about the money?"

Marga rummaged through her rucksack and produced the money.

The officer motioned and said gruffly, "He's in the back. I'll get him."

Sara didn't like the policeman at all. "You think Franz is all right?" she asked.

"I think so," Marga said, but she didn't look too sure.

Sara clasped her hands tightly, licked her lips, and listened intently. She could hear footsteps coming down the cement hall. She was suddenly aware of her long legs and gangly arms. Then there stood Franz, a stray lock of blond hair falling over his forehead, flinging his rucksack over his broad shoulder. He looked at Sara shyly and awkwardly shifted on his feet. "We'd about given up on you," he said, then looked away quickly. Sara blushed at Franz's uneasiness. Suddenly he grabbed her hand and squeezed it hard.

"Boy, am I ever glad to be out of that place," he said when they had crawled out of the underground prison. "The air was as stale as dry bread. And that jailer was a grouch."

Franz seemed confident now, and took the lead as they walked to the railroad station. He followed this path, then that, weaving his way through the maze of blockaded streets. Sara noticed that even in this burned-out city there were masses of people. Some were working around shelters ingeniously constructed of bits of brick, board, and tin. Others seemed to appear out of nowhere as they crawled out of basement shelters hidden somewhere beneath the debris. Many stood in slow-moving lines, waiting for a handful of potatoes.

The station looked like some angry giant had simply ripped out a wall. Steel rods jutted out threateningly from the remaining structure. The windows were patched with boards, and the door sagged on one bent hinge. But inside there were so many people that Sara found it difficult to walk. They sat listlessly on battered suitcases, lay curled up on the hard floor, or stood anxiously guarding their heap of belongings.

A train whistle cut through the lethargy, and the station came alive. As the train rumbled to a stop, the crowd rushed out the door and scrambled to get aboard.

"Come!" Franz urged them forward. "We have to get on."

The crowd pressed around them, and Sara felt like she could hardly breathe. Someone accidently swung a suitcase into the calf of her leg. "Hurry," Franz said, pulling at her hand. Sara could see that the back platform was starting to fill up. Then the conductor motioned for people to move away, and the train started to move slowly as its engine accelerated to a deafening roar.

Despair settled over the crowd. Sara sat down on her rucksack, put her head in her hands, and began to cry.

Marga shook Sara's shoulder. "Don't cry," she pleaded in a choked voice. "You're too big to cry." Sara sobbed even harder. Marga sat back and sighed. "Maybe we can get on tomorrow morning," she said more to herself than to Sara. "We'll stay here for the night—at least we're warm."

Sara sniffed and dried her eyes. "Do we have any more food?" she asked.

"No," Marga said. "But I think we might get some soup here. They fed us at the railroad stations when we were coming to get you."

"I hope so," Sara said. "I'm starved."

She looked around the room for some reassurance, but all she saw was the discouraged, glassy-eyed crowd. Suddenly she panicked. She didn't want to go to Hattorf. She just wanted to go back to the Children's Home, back where there was enough food and a warm bed. This felt too much like the trek, like being lost, like not having a home. She ran through the crowd and out the door. Then she stopped short. Up and down the street there was nothing was rubble—there was no place to go.

CHAPTER 8

The next day Sara stood crammed in a railroad car, held up on either side by Franz and Marga. People were pressed so tightly into the small space that she couldn't even turn around. Overhead, by the light bulb, was fastened a poem:

Please let the lightbulb screwed in tight
It gives us all such lovely light
To take it home won't help a bit
For neither volts nor socket fit.

"At least it has room up there, hanging all alone from the ceiling," Sara thought. She felt mashed, and her legs were so numb from standing in one position that they seemed to be part of the floor.

For two days they traveled. The cold invaded the unheated car and penetrated Sara's coat. The second night she managed to find a seat when they stopped at a station and people got off, but she slept fitfully, awakened by the stopping and starting of the train.

"Here's where we get off," Marga said when it was fully light. "Hattorf is about fifteen kilometers from here." Sara stretched and rubbed her eyes. Then she gathered up her sack, stepped off the train, and followed Franz. As they walked away from the city they also left the total destruction of the war. Sara noticed that in some small villages the houses were untouched, and she grew hopeful.

They had walked at least four hours when Franz stopped and pointed to a faraway figure. "It's Papa!" he shouted. "He's coming to meet us!"

Sara could see him, walking slowly along the dirt road. He leaned heavily on a cane.

"Papa, Papa!" Franz called, and ran to meet him.

Papa grabbed Franz's arm and quickened his pace. His cane dangled from his bent arm, and he held the other one out to Sara.

Suddenly they were in each other's arms. "Sara!" he said, his voice thick with emotion. "I thought we'd never find you." A tear fell on Sara's hair, and she could feel the quiet shaking of her father's body. He released her and put his stick on the ground. "Mama is waiting," he said. "Franz, run ahead and tell her that you're here."

But Franz had already gone, and Mama was coming quickly down the road to meet them. A slow shyness crept over Sara, and her steps shortened to a self-conscious shuffle. She brushed a curly lock of hair off her forehead and swung her ungainly arms nervously. She knew she was not the same little girl her mother had lost on the trek nearly a year ago.

Mama hugged her tightly, and Sara could feel the fast thumping of her mother's heart. Sara's eyes squinted with a smile, pushing the tears down her cheeks. "You've grown," Mama said, holding her at arm's length. Sara laughed and straightened to her full height. Perhaps Mama would understand after all.

"What took you so long?" Mama asked Franz. "You've been gone over two weeks. We've been worried sick. Papa paced the floor and walked to the road every day. We were afraid . . ." her voice trailed off.

As they walked inside the high-gabled farmhouse and up the narrow steps to their living quarters, Franz explained briefly about the traveling pass and his time in jail. Inside, Sara looked around the small room. In one corner stood a wood-burning stove. On its black surface sat a familiar wrought-iron kettle sending out a flavorsome smell. A rocking chair rested by the stove and three straight chairs stood lined up against the wall. Two beds, one on either side of the room, were spread with fluffy feather quilts. In the middle stood a small table.

"I suppose you're hungry," Mama said, taking a loaf of bread and slicing off thick, dark-brown pieces. Marga set the table, and Franz pulled a battered suitcase from under the bed. "I've been saving this special chair just for you," he joked, setting it on end for Sara.

When they were all seated around the table, mama brought a

bowl of steaming soup. Papa nodded, and they all bowed their heads in silence. When Sara raised her head, her mother's eyes were still closed, and her lips were moving inaudibly.

Sara looked around at everyone and smiled until her teeth showed and a happy sigh escaped. Mama's usually wistful eyes looked almost happy, and Papa's face was peaceful and relaxed. Sara felt almost too joyful to eat.

After supper Mama picked up some mending, and Papa sat rocking by the stove. "I won't have to walk to the road tomorrow," Papa said, "now that you've all come home."

Mama laid the mending in her lap and folded her hands. "I will turn their mourning into joy," she quoted, "and will comfort them and make them rejoice from their sorrow." Her eyes focused on Sara and traveled around the family circle. It was complete.

Days passed. Papa carved out new soles for his time-worn boots, and Franz worked on the farm. Mama baked bread and kept the family's few threadbare clothes clean and mended. Marga cooked and stood in line for their weekly rations of fat and flour. Sara was happy to be home, but she was restless. If only Liese were around to liven things up a bit. Out in the country here there was no one her age, and with nothing to do she was bored and a little lonesome.

"Would you like to learn to knit?" Mama asked, seeming to notice how Sara felt. She pulled out an old gray sweater that had been Sara's. "I kept it for you," she said. "I prayed that you'd be able to wear it again." She quickly handed it to Sara and looked away.

Sara unfolded the sweater and stuck her hand in the sleeve. It nearly reached her elbow.

"I knew it would be too small," Mama said, "but we can take it apart and use the yarn so you can make another one." She showed Sara how to unravel the tightly woven fabric and roll the yarn into a ball. When Sara had finished taking the sweater apart, she knelt beside her mother and watched carefully as her mother taught her how to cast on stitches. Slowly, she repeated each step, looping the yarn around the needle, first from the left and then from the right, after which she pulled the needle through and tightened the stitch. Gradually the needle filled with stitches, hugging the silver rod like beads on a string.

"My, you caught on easily," Mama said, looking at her work. Sara smiled and pulled the needle through to finish another row.

Now that there was something fun to do, Sara was content to be at home. Today she sat on the edge of the bed knitting. Franz was outside working, and Marga had left with a bag slung over her shoulder to pick up sticks for firewood. Papa was sleeping, and Mama sat on the rocking chair mending Franz's only pair of socks. Lately, it seemed that Papa slept all the time. Sara laid down her knitting and sprawled out on the bed. How sick was Papa? Last night he hadn't sat in the rocking chair. Sara missed that. When he did, Sara would sit on the floor close by the warm stove, and sometimes he would tell her stories about Russia. They weren't long stories because Papa wasn't a big talker. And they weren't scary stories, although Papa knew plenty of those from the Revolution. Sometimes she would ask him to tell about it, but he always changed the subject.

The quick pounding of footsteps on the stairs brought Sara out of her thoughts. Franz rushed into the room. "They took the Brauns!" he said between gasps for breath. "The Russians got them last night and sent them to Siberia."

Mama looked up quickly from her mending. "Who?" she asked, her voice tight with urgency.

"Isaac Braun," Franz said, his voice trembling. "They came last night and took the whole family."

Mama buried her head in her hands.

The Brauns. Sara remembered them from Steinfeld in Russia. She hadn't known they were living in Hattorf. But why were the Russians taking them to Siberia? This was Germany, and the war was over. She jumped off the bed and sat on the floor beside her mother.

"Dumb Ruskies," Franz said, and hit the table with his fist. "They think that just because of that lousy Yalta Agreement they can ship every person who ever came from Russia right back. All they want is people—people they can use for slaves in their horrible concentration camps."

He stopped and sank to the floor. A foreboding quiet hung over the room. "Mama, we can't stay here," he said finally. "We're too close to the Russian Zone."

Sara wiped the moisture from her hands and swallowed hard. A tense anger held her stiff, as if an iron rod had been driven

through her body. She had run and run and run—away from
Russia and Poland and the terrible war. Why, oh why couldn't she
stop? A tear trickled down her cheek. She huddled closer to the
stove, listening to the wind as it whipped around the corner of
the house. It seemed to her that even the wind was deliberately
trying to spoil the safety and comfort of their home. She stared
blankly at the cracked, brittle leather of her mother's shoe, and
tried to stay warm until Marga returned with more firewood.

It was a small amount of wood that Marga unloaded from her
rucksack an hour later. "There just isn't anything left," she said
wearily as she took the bag off her back. "Everyone's out picking
up what they can find." She looked around the room. "What's
wrong?"

A sharp knock on the door sent Sara scooting behind the stove.
Marga walked over and opened the door. "A letter for Frau
Friesen," the landlord said as he handed it to Marga.

"For me?" Mama asked, taking the letter. "Who could be
writing to us?" She tore open the envelope. "It's from Frau
Rempel," she said.

"Liese's mother?" Sara asked, coming out from behind the
stove.

"Yes." Mama scanned the letter, then read aloud slowly. "We
are in Gronau, a city near the Dutch border. Several Mennonite
men, Peter Dyck and Dr. Hylkema, have persuaded the Dutch
government to let Mennonite refugees into Holland on
something called a *Menno-Pass*. These men have promised the
government that the Dutch Mennonites and an organization
called the Mennonite Central Committee will take care of us. I
hope that you can come because I don't believe you are safe in
Hattorf. As you know, the Yalta Agreement says that all refugees
are to be sent back to their homeland. There are hundreds of us
waiting here at Gronau in an old army hospital. Just ask for the
Losserheim and you'll find us. —Frau Rempel."

Mama folded the letter with shaking hands and laid it in her
lap. "Papa's too sick to travel," she said softly.

"But the Russians," Franz argued. "We can't just stay here day
after day. They could come any night. This is our chance; can't
you see?"

Mama glanced over to the bed in the corner. "We can't move
Papa," she said in a whisper. "We will pray; that's all we can do."

CHAPTER 9

Papa was much worse. It seemed that Mama spent all of her time with him now—placing cool cloths on his head to lower the fever or feeding him hot soup.

Sara sat by the window, looking across the countryside. The wind spun the falling snow into a fury of swirling white, sending a blast of cold air through the windowpane. But still Sara stayed. It was beautiful the way the snow whitened the drab winter-brown earth and filled the few unsightly craters that defaced the countryside. She wished the snow would come and do the same thing for her. She felt as if a bomb had crashed into her soul, searing her flesh and ripping at the walls of her heart. Why was Papa always sick? Why couldn't he be well so they could have a happy family for once? Why couldn't they go to Gronau? His sickness always seemed to hang like a dark cloud over the family. Why? She propped her elbow against the windowsill and let the cold draft cool her face.

That night Sara wakened, gradually aware of hushed tones and candlelight. "Sara," Mama whispered, leaning over her bed. "Get up, Papa is worse."

Sara stood up quickly, pulled her blanket around her shoulders, and sat on the floor beside Papa's bed. Her eyes met his for an instant, and he reached out and took her hand. "At least I got to see my Sara again," he said faintly. He closed his eyes, and Sara felt his fingers relax. The stubby candle flamed higher for an instant and then nearly went out.

"He's gone," Mama said softly.

Gone? Sara stiffened and her head reeled. No, no, he couldn't be gone. How could he die? It was all her fault—all because she had been angry with him because he was sick. Oh, how could she have been so angry? She ripped herself away from the bedside, buried herself in her own soft bed, and cried.

The morning sun gradually lit up the small room. Sara lay perfectly still, burned out by guilt and tears.

"Sara?" It was Marga's voice.

Sara buried her head deeper in the covers. She didn't want anyone to talk to her. She had been absolutely horrible.

Marga sat on her bed in silence, holding her knees against her body, and propping her face on them. "Papa was really sick," she said finally. "The last trek out of Poland was more than he could take. It was so cold, and hardly any food. Well, it just was too much for him, being sickly the way he was."

Sara moved her head on the pillow and stared across the room. "No," she said in a flat voice, "it was my fault. I was angry at him for being sick."

"Why, Sara," Marga said with surprise, "how could you possibly think such a thing? He was sick."

"Well, I shouldn't have been angry at him."

"It was hard for all of us," Marga said, rubbing Sara's back. "Especially when we knew we couldn't go to Gronau. But that isn't why he died. He was sick—sick because his body simply wore out on the long trek and couldn't fight disease any longer."

Sara sat up in bed and looked straight at Marga. "I will miss him," she said thoughtfully.

"So will I," said Marga, tears filling her eyes. She threw her arms around Sara, and this time they cried together.

Early the next day Sara walked slowly behind the plain wooden box carried by Franz and Preacher Harder. Ahead she could see the snowy graveyard, with row upon row of small wooden crosses. She clutched the one she carried in her hand tighter. Yesterday she had spent the afternoon scratching her father's name deep into the wooden surface with a nail and rubbing soft coal into the cracks until the letters showed up clearly.

Their small procession stopped in front of a newly dug grave, and Preacher Harder opened his Bible. "I am the resurrection and the life. He who believes in me will live even though he dies," he read.

Sara looked down at the weathered wood of the box that held her father. How could he live again? She could still see his motionless body, feel his cold hands, and hear the echo of the

hammer as it pounded the coffin shut. What was real was the box being lowered into the ground and the thud of falling dirt covering it up. She held the cross in front of her face to cover her quivering lip and stiffened with irritating doubt. How could you believe anything you couldn't see?

Sara watched as Preacher Harder threw on the last shovelful of dirt, and then she stepped on the damp heap and pushed the cross deep into the loose soil. The wind tugged at it, but she held it upright and packed the earth around it firmly with her foot.

Gray clouds scuttled across the sky, and the trees bent their branches to the south. Sara turned up the collar of her coat and drew it around her more tightly. A sudden gust of wind caught the cross, and it wobbled and lay down. Franz picked it up and shoved it deeper into the ground.

"The wind sure is strong," Preacher Harder said, "and we can't even see it." He scanned the surrounding scene in silence.

Sara looked at him in bewilderment. The wind flapped the long gray coat around his legs and threatened to blow off his hat. It's true, she couldn't see the wind, but she could see what it was doing.

She leaned down and picked up a clod from her father's grave. She couldn't see Papa any more—the still cold body was under the black earth. But she could remember him—how he had urged them to flee and how he had hoped and suffered and rejoiced with them. That was what had made him Papa. And she had loved him and been angry with him and been lonesome for him. That brave, loving, and suffering Papa was still very real to her. She looked up at the fast-moving clouds and followed them across the sky. Then she crumbled the damp soil in her hand and let the loose earth sift through her fingers. For the last time, she straightened the cross and turned to follow her family home through the biting wind.

The house was silent. Mama sat on the rocking chair with her head lying against the back. Her black hair was pulled away from her high forehead, and her deep-set eyes were shut. Marga slowly stirred a pot of soup, and Franz lay on the floor absently whittling a stick to a point. Papa's coat hung on a peg, and his empty shoes sat beside the bed.

The soup was warm and thick. Mama ate slowly, her face expressionless. Franz kept his eyes on his bowl, and Marga picked out the potatoes and pushed the rest away.

Marga cleared the table, and Sara helped with the dishes. Mama rocked by the fire, her hands empty. Franz sprawled out beside her on the floor with his head propped up on an elbow and stared across the room.

"We might as well go to Gronau," Mama said, talking to no one in particular. Franz sat up. "Papa would have wanted us to go on," she said. "He was determined that we keep going—even when he could hardly keep on himself."

Franz stood up, put his hands in his pocket, and walked over to the window. Mama looked after him, and then got up and took Papa's coat off the hook. "I think it might fit you, Franz," she said, and held it out to him. Then she picked up the shoes, carried them over to the rocking chair, and began taking off her own battered boots. After stuffing the ends of Papa's big ones with paper, she put them on and settled back to rock. Her hands lay quietly in her lap.

Marga opened one of the cardboard suitcases and started packing. After a while Mama got up and mixed a batch of bread dough for the trip. Franz went searching for string to tie a suitcase shut. Mama's fists thumped and Marga's feet shuffled, breaking the empty stillness. Sara got up and started sweeping the floor.

The following morning dawned crisp and still. As the Friesens walked to the train station, carrying all their belongings in two suitcases and several backpacks, they passed the field of white crosses. They paused in silence, trying to record every detail of the orderly village graveyard. At the end of one row of crosses lay a mound of freshly turned earth. In the distance a train whistle blew, and the others walked on. But Sara stayed, with blurring eyes and aching throat. The whistle blew again, louder and longer. She raised her hand, waved a final good-bye, and walked toward the station.

CHAPTER 10

Sara stepped out into the fresh air and breathed deeply. It had been a long ride to Gronau, and the train had been over-crowded. "Where's the Losserheim?" Franz asked a railroad attendant.

"More refugees, I suppose," the man said in disgust. "We don't need any more of you folks. Pouring in here by the hundreds, you are, taking all our food when we have hardly enough to feed ourselves." He kicked at the floor. "Go straight north out of town. You can't miss it, surrounded by trees and all." He turned and walked away.

"What a grouch!" Franz said. "Come on, let's go."

Sara examined her shabby shoes, wishing they would swallow her up. The man had called them *refugees*— and the people in Gronau didn't want refugees. She slowly pulled her pack over her shoulder and trudged through town, looking down quickly every time she passed someone. Gradually the street narrowed and darkened as they entered a grove. A wooden sign marked LOSSERHEIM pointed to a long, low building. Sara quickened her pace. All she wanted to do was shut the door behind her and never come out. But Liese would be in there, and she couldn't be intimidated. Liese would flash her eyes and say, "What a grouch," just like Franz. The thought gave her courage.

It wasn't long until they had located Frau Rempel. "I'm so glad you came," she said, grasping Mama's hand. She motioned for her to sit on the bed. "Where's Heinrich?" she asked when she realized Papa was not with them.

"We buried him at Hattorf," Mama said, looking down at her hands.

"Oh, I'm sorry," Frau Rempel said, laying her hand on Mama's knee. They sat in silence—Sara felt her cheeks get hot and looked awkwardly around the large room for Liese. On either side, lined up against the wall, were high white beds. Here and there a person slept, but most people sat on the edges of the beds, waiting. Beside them stood small piles of assorted luggage— knapsacks, bundles, and suitcases in many sizes and conditions. Most of them were closed and ready.

"Tell me more about getting into Holland," Mama said, brushing her cheek.

"It's like I said in the letter," Frau Rempel explained. "Some Mennonites have come to help us. And they speak Low German just like we do. Peter Dyck, that's one of the men, lived in Russia when he was a boy, but his parents went to Canada during the Revolution. Now he's come back to help us.

"How's he going to help?" Franz broke in.

"Well, he's arranged with the Dutch government to allow Mennonites to cross over into Holland on a Menno-Pass. If you can speak Low German, you can get one. In Holland the Mennonites will take care of us and try to get us to another country."

"You mean like Canada?" Franz said, leaning forward expectantly.

"Yes," Frau Rempel said, and there was a glimmer of hope in her dark eyes. "It can't be too soon, either. There's just not enough food for a growing girl like Liese."

Canada—that's where Uncle Jakob lived. Sara remembered Papa talking about him. He had left Russia during the Revolution. She remembered Papa telling someone on the trek that he had been smart to get out when he did. She closed her eyes and tried to imagine what it would be like. They would have their own house with plenty of straw for their stove and a garden full of food. It would be in a peaceful village with a church, and they would never have to worry about the Russians. Yes, that's the way she would like it. Could Canada possibly be that way?

The bed suddenly jolted as Liese plopped herself beside Sara. "Hi," she said as she lay down. "The walk from school tired me out." Her pale face was thinner than Sara had remembered, and she looked as old as Marga. Two thin arms lay at her side, and her knees appeared like rocky bumps on her skinny legs. But that didn't seem as strange to Sara as the terse welcome and lifeless manner.

"You girls go get some lunch," Frau Rempel said.

Liese sat up. Her shoulders sagged wearily as she picked up the tin pail. "Come on," she said slowly. "I'll show you where it is."

They joined the long line forming in front of the mess hall. "Mama says we might go to Canada," Liese said, but her voice lacked the usual sparkle.

"Really?" Sara looked at her in admiration.

"My aunt lives there. She's got a car even."

"A car?" Sara wasn't sure she could believe that.

"Sure, everybody in Canada has a car."

"You're kidding," Sara said. Now she was sure that Liese was exaggerating in spite of her lethargy.

"No, I'm not!" Liese whined, breaking into tears. "My aunt wrote it in a letter."

Sara looked at her in bewilderment. Liese had never been so sensitive before.

"What else did she write?" she asked, sorry that she had disagreed.

"Oh, they have fields full of wheat, and all the good white flour they want, and the children go to school and learn to talk English, and they heat their houses with coal, and they're never cold."

"Really?" Sara asked. She wondered what that would feel like, but she didn't have time to wonder long because Liese was holding up her tin pail and the cook was filling it with steaming soup. Liese walked slowly, holding the pail so she didn't spill even one drop over the side.

When they returned, Frau Rempel carefully dipped an equal amount of soup into an assortment of empty tin cans. She gave the only dishes to Mama and Marga. Sara looked into her half-filled can and looked around the room guiltily. "You take all our food away," she heard the railroad man saying. She knew the cans would be full if the Rempels hadn't been sharing with them.

Frau Rempel bowed her head. "Segne Vater diese Speise, uns zur Kraft und Dir zum Preise." Sara relaxed. She dipped into her soup with her finger, touching the one tiny piece of turnip, and followed it around the edge of the can until she could pick it out and eat it. Then she tipped the can to her lips and drank the watery broth. Liese was still slowly sipping hers. When she finished it, she stared into the empty can with wistful eyes, and Sara knew she was still hungry. Maybe that was why she seemed so tired and listless.

It wasn't long until Sara's family had settled into life at the Losserheim. They had parked their belongings beside some empty beds and stacked up the suitcases for a table. They had also received their ration cards from the city, but that didn't provide nearly enough food. Even on a full card there was hardly enough to eat, but when they had come to Gronau the rations had been cut in half. "Sorry, lady," the clerk had told Marga, "but you refugees are just piling up here in hope of crossing the border, and we have to discourage it somehow." There was a tin of soup every meal and a little bread, but that was all.

The scanty fare filled Sara's stomach like a pebble thrown into a cavern. She was listless and felt so dizzy whenever she stood up that she didn't even feel like playing with Liese. Images of thick soup and heavy bread filled her thoughts, but mealtimes only teased her appetite. Marga was cross, and Mama lay down most of the time. Franz was sullen and silent. If only they could get across into Holland, there would be food. They had come to Gronau just in time, because the Mennonite refugees had started to cross the border as fast as the officials could process them.

Maybe tomorrow it would be their turn.

But the boredom was broken sooner than Sara expected. "Peter Dyck, Peter Dyck is here," the message rushed from room to room. "Meet in the assembly room." There was a sudden hustle of activity as the war-weary people moved quickly to the large room.

A stranger with light, wavy hair and deep-set eyes stood before them. "Good morning," he said, gesturing with his hat. "I'm Peter Dyck. My job this morning is not a pleasant one because I come with bad news." He paused, and Sara could see that he was gripping his hat so hard that his knuckles were white. "The border has been closed. The Russians found out that the Dutch government was letting us into their country, and that made them very angry. They, of course, want you all back in Russia." Sara caught her breath and tensed. "The Russians have put so much pressure on the Dutch government that they've decided to stop allowing us to cross the border. You see, some Dutch soldiers are still in Russia, and they've threatened not to let them come home if we are allowed to keep entering Holland. I've done everything I can do."

A deathly silence fell over the room. No one moved. Sara stared at Peter Dyck with glazed eyes until he became a blur. She wished she could cry, but she felt too rigid inside. In fact, the whole roomful of people stood as motionless as hollow statues.

Then a firm voice broke the spell, "We must continue to pray!"

Sara could see her mother bow her head, and Peter Dyck's strong voice took up the suggestion: "Our great God is still our refuge and strength; he is ever aware of our problems and fears. Thus we have no business doubting him, even though God's earth is wrapped in tragedy. God continues to reign as all-wise and as almighty as ever. His eternal plan is not canceled out by the whims of men. God is here among us; he continues to be our refuge and strength."

Sara soaked up the words like a sponge takes in water. They entered the dark emptiness and filled it with hope. She stood silently, surrounded by a peace that defied the horrible news.

CHAPTER 11

Sara stood by the window, staring at the crossing gate that controlled the international border. It would not open for her. She had come over two thousand kilometers, much of it on foot or horse-drawn wagon, only to find a closed gate. Her stomach hurt, and her mind wandered to the big wooden barrel that had stood in their pantry in Russia. It was full of round, red tomatoes floating in a salty brine. She remembered the kitchen and imagined herself sitting down to a warm bowl of borscht full of cabbage, potatoes, and ham. A pitcher of thick cream stood beside it, and she poured it into the steaming broth. Her stomach growled and gnawed at nothing but its own juices.

Sara took one last look out of the window and went back to her family. Franz was scowling and pounding his leg to make a point. Mama looked upset. "I don't care," Franz said in a harsh whisper. "I'm not going to sit here and starve."

"All right, then, do what you have to do," Mama said reluctantly. Franz got up and walked out of the room, and Mama watched him go.

"What's he going to do?" Sara asked in an alarmed voice.

"Nothing," Mama answered firmly, and Sara knew that she didn't dare ask again.

"You might as well go to school tomorrow," Mama said, straightening herself as she turned toward Sara. "I've heard that they have a child-feeding program there."

Sara's eyes grew big and her hands shook. Food! In her mind she could see a thick slice of rye bread topped with a slab of firm yellow cheese. Her mouth watered and her head felt light. "Liese has gone before, so you can go with her," Mama added. But Sara scarcely heard her. Tomorrow she would have food.

The school was a two-story brick building. Sara followed Liese up the steps and into her new classroom. "The teacher's mean," Liese warned her, and quickly went to take her seat. Herr Mueller looked up from his work, pushed his glasses up on his nose and glared at Sara.

"New?" he asked. Sara nodded. "Your name?"

"Sara Friesen," she said softly, looking at the floor.

"Refugee, I suppose?" he sneered.

Sara's shoulders dropped. "Yes, sir," she answered in a whisper.

"Speak up, I can't hear you."

"Yes, sir," she repeated. Her mouth was dry and her voice scratchy.

"Take a seat in the back," he said with a motion toward a makeshift bench against the back wall.

Sara walked stiffly to the back and sat down. Next to her, a girl pulled her skirt together and scooted down the bench away from Sara. Across the room even Liese sat with her head bowed, looking as small as Sara felt.

"Sara Friesen, can you divide?" Herr Mueller stood with his arms folded, waiting for an answer.

Sara winced. "No, sir," she said, standing quickly.

"Just what I thought," he muttered under his breath. "Can you add and subtract?"

"Yes, sir."

"Multiply?"

"A little, sir."

"Well, you'd better learn—and fast. We don't have time to wait around on ignorant refugees."

Sara lowered her eyes, and although her body sat on the hard bench, her mind drifted out of the room.

"Sara!" Herr Mueller's voice jolted her back.

She jumped to her feet. "Ye-e-es, sir," she stammered.

"Well, what is it?"

Her eyes darted from side to side. What could she say? She hadn't heard the question. "I-I don't know, sir." Several children beside her snickered. She sat down slowly and tried to listen, but inside she rebelled. She would never come back again. Never!

At recess time, Sara glanced uncertainly around the room. Liese was already toward the front of the line of children preparing to go outside. Herr Mueller had his back turned. Sara walked up to Liese and stepped in line behind her.

Outside they filed past a massive kettle of porridge which a woman ladled into tin cans. Sara took her can with great care and reverently dipped her spoon into the creamed wheat. It felt smooth and thick on her tongue as she turned it over and over in her mouth, trying to make each spoonful last as long as she could. "This is the only reason I come," Liese said.

Sara nodded her head and licked her lips. She would keep coming for this. Each rounded spoonful made up for the unpleasant morning.

Even with the daily porridge, Sara was always hungry. The very thought of food made her mouth water and sent her mind spinning—how could she get it? She had overheard Marga saying that Franz was crossing the border at night for food—that was why Mama had been so upset. She resolved to ask him about it, then grew fearful and thought about telling Liese to do it. No, she decided, this time she was going to make something happen herself. A tingle of fear ran down her spine, but she shook it off with a quick movement of her shoulder.

"Yes," Franz admitted when Sara asked. But he was surprised when Sara asked if she could go along. "Why, you're just a girl, and only twelve at that."

"Please," Sara pleaded. "I have to get food."

Franz straightened himself and looked at the long skinny arms and legs that looked like an assortment of bones standing upright. "H-m-m. It's very dangerous, you know. The sign at the border says anyone who crosses illegally will be shot on sight. Really sure you want to?"

Sara nodded deliberately, but her heart pounded. "I have to get food," she repeated.

"I know," Franz said and dropped his hands limply at his side. "It's not fair—all that food right over the border and here we are starving." His voice grew louder and his mouth closed tightly. "I'm not going to sit here with an empty stomach when there's food within a few hundred meters."

"Neither will I," Sara said firmly.

"All right, but are you sure Mama will let you go?"

"You ask her," Sara said. "I'm scared."

"I won't take anyone who's scared."

That decided it—she would ask. She sat beside her mother for a long time, watching her patch a hole in a sweater with a little bit of yarn she had gotten by shortening the sleeves. "Mama, can I go across the border with Franz tonight?" she finally blurted out.

"What?" Mama asked in a shocked voice, putting down her knitting.

"Franz said I could. I have to get food. Please, Mama."

Mama looked up and down Sara's thin body, and a hurt look came to her eyes. "I can't let you go," she said softly.

"I have to have food," Sara insisted. Her empty stomach gnawed painfully, and she clenched her fists. "Mama, I'm hungry," she begged.

Mama closed her eyes, and Sara could see the deeply etched lines around her mouth. "You may go. But be careful," she said finally.

"Thank you, Mama," she said, laying her head on her mother's shoulder. "I *will* be careful."

That night, a full moon hung in the late autumn sky, lighting their way. They turned off the main road and walked silently through the woods, making sure to circle around the patrol building that controlled the border crossing. The trees cast long shadows and blocked out the moon. Sara followed close to Franz, hanging onto the back of his coat. Suddenly he stopped and Sara rammed into his bony back—a fallen tree blocked the way. Franz scrambled up and then reached down to help Sara.

They jumped off the tree and paused to rest. Sara was glad for the chance to catch her breath, but all too soon Franz motioned for her to follow. Soon the trees thinned, the moon came into full view, and they returned to the road.

"Now," Franz said, "you're on your own. Think you can find your way back?"

Sara nodded and tried to act confident even though her legs grew weak and her hands trembled. Ahead, a single light flickered. She swallowed hard and walked toward it.

The light led her to a farmhouse. Sara looked back to see if anyone was following, then rapped at the door. A small woman, wiping her hands on her apron, opened the door while a toddler hung onto her leg and peered around her skirt. Sara looked down at her feet. "May I have some food?" she asked in a small voice.

"Come on in," the woman said, picking up the little one. "Sit down. My, you look starved. Did you come over the border?"

Sara hesitated. "It's all right," the woman reassured her. Sara nodded her head. A girl of about six leaned on the table looking at Sara with wide-eyed wonder. "All by yourself?" she asked.

"With my brother," Sara explained, but she felt proud that she hadn't depended on Liese.

"Weren't you scared?"

"Hush," said her mother, as she set the tot on the floor. "Don't be so nosy." She placed a pot on the stove and began to slice a loaf of bread. "I have to get this girl some food."

And food it was. Sara dipped her spoon into the heavy stew, marveling with each bite at the large pieces of meat, potatoes, and carrots. Then there was a large slice of bread, a hunk of cheese, and a full glass of milk.

Sara put down her spoon and bit into the mellow cheese, feeling it crumble into sharp-tasting morsels. When every crumb was gone, she picked up the glass of milk. It was cool and velvety on her tongue and left a thickness in the back of her throat. She reached for the bread, paused to pick up the spoon, and then laid it down to grab the glass. There was so much food she didn't know which to eat first!

"Are you always this hungry?" the woman asked.

Sara stopped eating and nodded her head. Perhaps she was only dreaming again. Quickly she grabbed the slice of bread, fearing it would suddenly disappear.

The woman sat down on a chair next to Sara. "It must be hard for a growing girl to always be hungry. Is there anything you could do—like knit mittens for the children or something—in exchange for food?"

Sara blinked hard and laid down the bread. 'Wha-a-t?" she stammered, then added, "Yes, I mean, I knit."

"Wonderful," the woman said, getting up. "I'll give you some yarn, and when you're done with a pair of mittens, bring them back and I'll give you another meal."

Sara smiled so big that she had to laugh. Her body felt light, and she wanted to run around the room and shout for joy. But instead she filled her spoon and ate until she felt full.

"Better put this under your coat," the woman said as she started unwinding the yarn. "If you get caught smuggling it across the border, you'll be in trouble." She wrapped it around Sara's waist, buttoned Sara's coat over it, and checked the heavy fabric for tell-tale lumps. "Can't see a thing," the woman assured her. "See you in a few nights from now."

"Thank you," Sara said in a loud, clear voice.

She crept back through the dark woods, over the border, and down the moonlit streets of Gronau. Tomorrow she planned to tell Liese all about it.

CHAPTER 12

Liese was impressed with Sara's successful crossing and soon was going into Holland herself. It made Sara proud to have been able to show Liese something for once. Two months later, Sara was still sneaking across the border several nights a week. Tonight she was going to baby-sit for the children. She walked quickly through the cold night air. The firm path under her feet told her she was going in the right direction even though the moon had gone under a cloud and the trees were nothing but black shapes in the night shadows. A lonely quiet filled the forest, and her plodding footsteps echoed loudly through the dark stillness.

"Stop!" a commanding voice shouted. "Who's there?"

Sara stopped and stiffened. A light was sweeping the area. She looked around with panic, trying to find a place to hide. Right beside her was the fallen tree. She ducked, crawled to it, and pressed herself against the damp piece of rotting wood. The footsteps were coming nearer, and she could see the light bobbing only a few meters away. Her arm was twisted in an uncomfortable position, but she didn't dare move. The light came toward her and beamed brightly on the tree. Now she could hear breathing, and a shoe nearly stepped on her. Suddenly there was a loud crash and an angry curse as someone stumbled headlong over the log and landed on the other side.

"I've had enough for tonight," a man muttered angrily as he picked himself up. He walked a few steps, then shone his light up and down the path. "There's a path here all right. Someone's coming across. Just wait, I'll get them another night." He spat on the ground and walked off into the darkness.

Sara lay perfectly still until the footsteps faded away and the light disappeared completely. Then she sat up. Her arm ached, her mouth felt gritty, and her face was dirty and scratched. She sat quietly a little longer, then stood up and turned toward home. She walked slowly, lifting her feet carefully and setting them down like a cat stalking prey. Never had the path seemed so long and tedious—the moon shone and then disappeared again, and still she was surrounded by trees. Finally, she saw the clearing. She ran as fast as she could, not stopping until she reached the Losserheim, and flopped down on her bed.

"What's wrong?" Mama asked in a concerned voice.

Sara put her hand on her chest, gasped for air, and shook her head to indicate that she couldn't talk just yet.

Her mother unbuttoned her coat and poured some water in a basin to wash her dirty, scratched face. Sara lay quietly until she caught her breath and then she started to cry.

She woke up the next morning with her coat still on and a blanket spread over her. "Are you all right?" her mother asked when she saw that she was awake.

"What happened?" Franz asked. "You still haven't told us."

When Mama heard the story her face turned white and she rubbed her hands on her dress. "No more," she said, and her voice sounded final.

Franz looked at her and his mouth turned down in a determined scowl. "I'll find another way," he said.

Mama's eyes registered fear, but she said nothing. She turned to Sara and repeated, "You may not go anymore."

"I know," Sara murmured. But inside she felt desperate. How would she get food? Besides, she knew Liese would keep on going anyway. The thought only made her feel worse.

The days dragged slowly by, unmarked by the thick Dutch stew. Sara grew steadily thinner. It was becoming more and more difficult for her to remember her number facts, and Herr Mueller had no patience. "Typical refugee," he would mutter, "can't learn a thing." Sara heard what he said, but she was too tired to feel angry. He could say anything he wanted as long as she got her daily bowl of porridge.

Marga had found work at the Van Deldon textile mill. That meant that now there was a little money. But money was almost worthless since the war, and food could be gotten only with coupons. Occasionally, though, one could buy herring fish with money. Today as Sara walked home from school, she fantasized about the salty-sour taste of the herring. Perhaps Mama had been able to get some today.

As she approached the Losserheim she was surprised to see a large crowd of people gathered outside. She walked faster, scanning the group for her mother. When she saw her, she wiggled through the mass and grabbed her mother's arm. "What's going on?" she asked.

"They're giving away food."

Sara stood on tiptoe and craned her neck to see a man and woman standing in front of a truck handing out parcels. Sara looked at the packages, trying to figure out how many there were. "What if there aren't enough?" she worried.

Suddenly the badge on the woman's coat sleeve caught her eye. On a white circular patch, two hands clasped in friendship across the vertical beam of a blue cross. Around the circle was lettering that read "Mennonite Central Committee." Sara poked her mother excitedly. "They're Mennonites!" she whispered. Her very own people!

Sara took her eyes from the patch as she realized that her mother was reaching for a package. "We'll be back next week," the woman said with a smile as she handed her a brown parcel.

Sara grabbed the bundle and hurried back to the room with unusual vigor. Her hands trembled as she tried to open the heavy wrapping. "Don't ruin the paper," Mama warned. Sara pulled at it but her fingers were as uncooperative as if they had been toes. "Here, you do it," she said, pushing it across the bed to Mama.

Mama peeled off the paper, picked out a small, flat package, and handed it to Sara. Clumsily, Sara slipped off the outer paper and unwrapped the thin aluminum covering. A chocolate bar! She broke off one section and bit into the soft, sweet square that melted in her mouth. She put the remaining chocolate back, and then looked questioningly at her mother. Her mouth watered, and she desperately wanted to eat the whole thing.

"It's yours," Mama said. "Franz is still getting across to Holland, and Marga isn't a growing girl." She picked up a small sack and tore open a corner to peek at the contents. "Sugar," she announced. "And here's a can of milk, some coffee, and a box of cigarettes. They must have bought up some old army supplies." She stared at the odd assortment of things in silence. "Perhaps we can trade the coffee and cigarettes for some flour," she said finally. "Then I could bake a cake."

But Sara's mind wasn't on a cake. She bit into the brown chocolate and ate it all.

Every Wednesday Sara walked home from school a little faster so that she could be there when the MCC truck came. There still wasn't very much food, but it was something. Now Sara wasn't *always* hungry, and she was less tired and listless. As Mama said, "We don't have enough to get fat on, but we have enough to survive."

They weren't fat—that is, nobody except Frau Fast. Nobody cared that Frau Fast was heavier than the rest, but what they did care about was that she always made it her business to answer the door when the MCC people came.

"How do they know we hardly have enough to keep alive?" Franz complained after Peter Dyck and another MCC man, Siegfried Janzen, had come for a visit. "All they ever see is Frau Fast, and she looks like she gets plenty to eat."

"We have to figure out a way of keeping her from answering the door," Marga said. "But that's going to be hard to do. She thinks it's her job."

"Her job!" Franz sniffed. "It's her job to stay out of sight."

"Franz!" Mama scolded.

"Oh, all right," Franz said, "but I still think we should keep her from answering the door."

Sara didn't say anything, but she told Liese about it later. Liese suggested that they keep on the lookout for MCC men and do everything they could to get someone to the door before Frau Fast.

Next day, on their way home from school, Sara and Liese saw a familiar car pull up beside the front door of the Losserheim. They raced home, reaching the building just as the men got out of the car. Sara's heart pounded and she felt dizzy. Liese went in the side door with Sara close at her heels, but the door slammed shut too quickly, caught Sara's heel, and sent her sprawling on the floor. Her head thumped from running, and she was completely exhausted. She moved her head to look at her stinging knee. It was skinned, and blood was trickling down her leg.

Just then the door opened and Frau Fast stepped in. "I have to stop her," Sara thought desperately. She grabbed her knee and let out a loud "O-w-w!"

Frau Fast stopped for a minute and looked down at her. "What's the matter?" she asked in a husky voice.

"I fell coming through the door and hurt my knee," she moaned. "Can you help me?"

Frau Fast looked at the knee and then urgently down the hall toward the front door. "I don't know," she said, her voice hesitant with indecision. "The MCC men just came!"

"Please," Sara pleaded. "It really hurts."

Frau Fast took another look at the bleeding knee. "All right," she said. "Here, I'll help you walk to my room and bandage it up. Someone else can answer the door."

Down the hall Sara could see Liese grab her mother's arm and then Frau Rempel quickly move to answer the front door. She breathed a sigh of relief.

"Oh, there you are," Liese said, nearly bumping into them. She pointed to the front door and shouted, "We did it!" Then she saw Frau Fast. "Oh," she gasped, and covered her mouth. She turned and fled in the opposite direction. Sara's ears grew hot, and she looked at the floor.

Frau Fast poured some water and gently washed Sara's knee, then tore a precious piece of white cloth for a bandage.

"I had wanted to see if the MCC men had been able to get any medicine for me," she said as she wrapped Sara's knee. She panted as she talked, and Sara could see her puffy eyes and doughy skin. Her own empty stomach suddenly seemed minor compared to the obvious sickness of the large woman. She hung her head and said, "Thank you" in a very small voice. When she left Frau Fast's room the hall was noisy with excitement, but Sara couldn't be glad. Frau Fast would go another week without medicine.

Sara found her mother talking to Frau Rempel. "Did you hear what Peter Dyck and Siegfried Janzen came for?" Liese's mother asked. "They're coming to Gronau to set up a Mennonite refugee camp."

Sara's eyes opened wide and her face lit up. Maybe now there would be all the food they wanted! And Frau Fast would have her medicine.

/

CHAPTER 13

Sara picked up a suitcase and followed Franz out the door. Today was moving day for the Friesens. They were going to live in a large public house called the *Schützenhof,* one of three buildings the MCC had acquired for the refugees. Sara thought it was the loveliest building she had ever seen. Sunlight gleamed on the red tile roof and in the yard a tree was white with blossoms. They entered the door hesitantly and set down their luggage.

"Welcome to the Mennonite Refugee Camp," Siegfried Janzen said, holding out his hand in welcome. "Follow me, and I'll show you where you can stay." He led them down the hall and

into a large room divided by rows and rows of hanging blankets. At the other end of the room, high on the wall, was a semicircular window, flooding the room with light. Above him huge wooden beams arched to the top of a high ceiling. He led them through the maze of hanging blankets until they came to an open space. "Here we are," he said, pointing to a pair of bunk beds. "There are blankets on the beds that you can hang up for some privacy. A bell will ring for lunch—just go around the corner to the kitchen and get your food. You may eat here in your room."

"I get a top bunk," Sara said when he had left.

"I get the other one," Franz said, "but first we have to figure out how to hang these blankets." To the left, one blanket was already hung by the neighboring family, and since they were located against one wall of the large room, two sides were left to be enclosed.

"There's a line to hang them on," Marga said, pointing to the wire overhead that outlined their small space. Mama and Marga threaded pieces of heavy string through at equal distances along the blankets. Then Sara crawled on a top bunk and tied the blankets to the wire while Franz held them.

Their very own room! A bunk bed sat on either side with a meter's width between them. From where Sara sat on her top bunk she could see right into the next bedroom. A young woman rocked a small baby, and a grandmother bounced a toddler on her knee. The child looked up and pointed at Sara. "Girl! Girl!" he shouted. Sara lay down quickly on her bed. "Where did the girl go?" she heard the child ask.

"Shhh," said the grandmother.

Marga had piled up the suitcases against the back wall and covered them with a beautiful white tablecloth. Sara could still remember the smooth linen spread over their table in Russia. When it was on the table, Sara knew that someone special was coming for a meal. Now its fringed edge hung halfway down the makeshift pile, hiding the ugly brown suitcase.

"Let me get something," Sara said, tugging at a suitcase on the bottom.

"What do you want now?" Marga said in an exasperated voice. "I've just got everything arranged."

Sara continued to pull on the suitcase. Suddenly it came, sending her back on the floor with a thud and the suitcases clattering in every direction. The baby in the next room started to cry.

"See what you did?" Marga shouted.

"Quiet!" Mama whispered sternly. "They can hear us through the blanket."

Sara opened the suitcase, pulled out a small black and white photograph, and handed it to Marga. "I wanted to get this," she explained.

"Oh," Marga said quietly. She looked at the picture of a man with balding hair and a thick mustache.

Sara didn't want to look at Mama, so she started putting the makeshift table back together again. "There didn't seem to be any place to put it before," she said lamely, propping Papa's picture against the wall. No one said anything, and the silence was heavy and painful. Sara folded her hands and swallowed hard. She was sorry she had gotten the picture out.

Before she could put it away, the dinner bell rang and Franz jumped up to get the food. Sara brightened and looked at the picture. Perhaps it could be in the room after all.

"Open the door," Franz called from the other side of the blanket.

"Door?" Sara said, and then surprised herself by laughing.

"All right, then, open the blanket," he said, as Sara drew it back.

There was soup—not too thin—and cornbread. Sara bit into the cornbread, but her teeth hardly dented it. So she dunked it into her soup until it softened.

"I wonder what we're going to have for supper," Marga said.

Sara chewed her cornbread and sighed. The soup was warm and her stomach was almost full. To be able to wonder about supper seemed almost too good to be true.

"How about cornbread rocks dunked in soup?" Franz suggested.

Marga smiled and Franz chuckled. But Sara was too busy eating to smile.

That evening they walked through the fresh spring air to the clubhouse where the refugees from the three MCC houses met for evening worship. Even though they were an hour early, the room was already half full. Just in time to join in the preservice singing, they settled themselves on the boxes they had carried along for makeshift seats. Herr Bergen stood up and lined out the first phrase, *"Nun danket alle Gott mit Herzen, Mund und Händen."* The congregation echoed back in a full sound that filled the room to the very corners. "Now thank we all our God with hearts and hands and voices." Herr Bergen's deep voice lined out the second phrase, and again there was a mighty burst of praise as everyone joined in singing. "Who wondrous things hath done, in whom His world rejoices." The words rushed out, carried on the sound of hundreds of voices united in worship.

Joy and pride welled up in Sara like an expanding balloon. She belonged to something stronger than war, bigger than hunger, and more beautiful than a peaceful village. Afterwards, as they walked down the dark street to the *Schützenhof*, she decided that she would come every night.

Spring turned into summer. Sara no longer had to face the daily taunts of Herr Mueller at school, and she had enough food. Her sunken cheeks had begun to fill out and regain their old color. Now when she undressed it was harder to count each individual rib, and she didn't always feel tired. The days were warm, and since the tiny room was hot and stuffy and the toddler in the next room seemed to whine all day, Sara and Liese often went outside.

Today the front yard was covered with bedding that had been laid out to be aired. Under a tree, their mothers sat with a group of women carefully unraveling the stitching from the flour sacks. "Go get us some more sacks," Liese's mother said when she saw the girls. "David and some other boys are in the back shaking them for us."

Liese grabbed Sara's arm and giggled self-consciously. David lived in the room next to Liese, and for some reason she always acted silly when she talked about him. They walked to the back of the building, but the boys were facing the other direction and didn't notice them. "David's all covered with flour, David's all covered with flour," Liese taunted.

Suddenly David turned and cracked the sack right in the girls' faces. Sara ducked, let out a surprised yelp, and ran to the side of the building only to fall headlong over Liese. There they lay in a pile, their faces streaked white with powdery flour. Sara started to giggle.

Liese got up quietly, crept up to the corner, and peeked

around. Crack!—another bag whipped in her direction. She ducked behind the wall, covering her mouth to muffle her giggles. "You look next," she told Sara.

Cautiously, Sara peered around the corner. Another bag whizzed through the air. "Oh," Sara yelled, and flattened herself against the wall. Her breath came in short gasps and she started to hiccup.

Two bags dropped on the ground in front of them. "They're all done," a voice yelled. "Take them."

Sara picked up the bags, and she and Liese dashed around the building to where the women were working. She threw the bags on her mother's lap. "Wait a minute," Mama said, "we need someone to roll up the thread." She handed Sara a stick and showed her how to wrap the unraveled thread around it so it didn't tangle. Sara sat on the ground and hiccupped loudly. Liese started to giggle. "My, what's got into you girls?" Mama asked.

"I don't know," Frau Rempel said with a smile, "but it does my heart good to see them laughing." Her hands moved deftly, folding a finished sack, then rubbing it smooth long after all the wrinkles were gone. "There were times I was afraid they would never laugh again."

The women were suddenly quiet, and Sara looked up in time to see her mother's eyes moisten with tears. She looked down and started to wind the thread as fast as she could. Mama cried a lot now. Sara didn't understand, but she liked it better than when Mama was so painfully quiet.

The women's talk wandered to the future. One woman had decided to go to Paraguay because she knew her aging mother couldn't pass the medical exam. Frau Rempel was planning to go to her sister in Canada—the one with the car, Sara thought immediately, and felt happy for Liese. Mama was silent.

"What about you?" one of them asked her.

"Do you have a sponsor?" another one wanted to know.

Sara stopped winding and looked at her mother. She had never heard of a sponsor.

"The MCC workers are trying to locate Heinrich's brother Jakob, but they haven't had much success yet," said Mama. "We think that he's in Canada."

There was a sudden lull in the conversation, and Sara could almost hear the thump of her quickening heartbeat. "What's a sponsor?" she asked her mother in a whisper.

"It's someone who will pay our way and get us settled," her mother answered. "It's about the only way for our family to get to Canada."

"Oh," Sara said flatly. "What if we can't find a sponsor?"

"Then we'll go to Paraguay," she said. "It's one of the few countries that will take us besides Canada."

Sara was quiet for a long time. "Why can't we stay here?" she wondered.

"We're just refugees," Mama explained. "We can only stay until we are allowed to enter some other country."

Refugee! Sara hated the word. Would she ever find a place that was really home?

CHAPTER 14

Winter had come to Gronau. Snow came in white streaks toward the windowpane and stacked up in the corners, but inside the *Schützenhof* there was nothing but excitement. The children were getting ready for Christmas.

It was Sara's turn with the scissors. She cut along the folds in her paper, making long narrow strips, and then handed the scissors to her neighbor. When it was her turn for the red crayon she pressed hard on each strip in order to get it as colorful as possible. Then she dipped one end into the gooey flour-water paste, formed it into a circle, and pressed the two ends together. Threading the next strip through the circle, she repeated the process until she had formed a small red chain. When they had everyone's chains joined it would go around the tree several times.

Sara put her chain down and silently recited her poem. She knew it so well she didn't even have to pause. It would be all right for the program tomorrow night. After school they would practice their songs one last time, and then everything would be ready. She tingled with excitement. The only Christmas program she could remember had been back in Russia when she was only seven years old.

Would there be Christmas in Canada? What if Uncle Jakob had died and they could never reach him? She pushed the thought aside and fingered her paper chain—it felt waxy smooth and very real. The future could wait until after Christmas.

The day of the program seemed to drag by as Sara waited for evening to come. She said her poem over and over and hummed the songs. At last supper was finished and everyone was ready to go.

When Sara walked into the assembly room she stopped short and looked around in awe. A large tree shining with candles gave the entire room a magic glow. On its branches hung the paper chain and right in front was an especially bright red strip that she was sure was hers. Her eyes glowed, and there was a spring in her step as she walked to the front and took her place with the other children.

"This is a special Christmas," Peter Dyck said as he opened the program, "a Christmas when we realize that God has brought us safely through the most terrible war the world has ever known. Let us thank him for this wonderful gift in silent prayer."

Sara closed her eyes and then opened them a crack to look at the beautiful tree. She smiled and squeezed her hands tightly.

"Another tree!" Sara exclaimed later when they arrived at another building for the Christmas party.

"And look at the presents!" Liese said loudly, then lowered her voice. "Do you suppose they are for us?"

Sara stared in disbelief. She sat down on a nearby bench and slid toward the middle. Not once did she take her eyes off the tree.

"These are gifts from children in the United States and Canada," Peter Dyck said, picking up a bundle. "Some boy or girl

just your age bought some things they thought you might need, wrapped them in a towel, and sent them to Germany for you. On the front of the bundle is a label that tells you who sent it, where they live, and how old they are." He held the bundle closer for a better look. "This one is for Sara Friesen. Sara, will you come forward?"

Sara sat fastened to her chair, her heart beating wildly.

"Sara Friesen," he said again, "are you here?"

"Go!" Liese said in a loud whisper and gave her a push.

Slowly and with her shoulders sagging self-consciously, Sara stood up and walked to the front. Herr Dyck placed a snow-white bundle in her arms, and somehow Sara managed a hoarse "Thank you" and returned to her seat.

"What's in it?" Liese demanded.

"I want to see what it says," Sara said, irritated at Liese's impatience. She rubbed her hand over the soft white towel, then ran her index finger over the stitching that fastened the label to it. "From Jane Miller, Waterloo, Ontario, Canada, Age 12." In the corner was the familiar MCC symbol and at the bottom, in large letters, was printed "IN THE NAME OF CHRIST."

"Hurry," Liese said. "I want to see what's in it."

Sara turned the package over, unfastened the four safety pins that held it together, and unfolded it. Then she gasped and put her hands to her mouth, for there lay a beautiful red and green plaid skirt.

"There's something underneath," Liese said, pulling at a dark green sleeve.

Sara lifted the skirt, and Liese grabbed a lovely green sweater. A patch of red clung to the dark wool. "Look," Sara exclaimed, "new socks!"

Something clattered to the floor, and a hand from behind grabbed it. "David!" Liese whispered loudly.

"What's this?" he asked, waving a six-inch tube.

"I don't know," Liese said, grabbing it.

"Wait," David said, putting his head close to Liese's. "It says something here on the tube—C-O-L-G-A-T-E. I've never heard of that—must be English."

Liese giggled and tried to pronounce it.

"Here's something else," Sara said, holding up a small paper package. She pulled off the paper and found a hard white block.

"Soap," she said, lifting it to her nose. "And it smells good." She set it down and picked up one last thing—a small black book. "A Bible!" she exclaimed. "A Bible of my very own."

Ever so slowly, Sara stacked her gifts in a pile, wrapped them in the towel again, and pinned it shut. Never had she had so many beautiful things and never had she felt so much like she belonged.

When everyone had received a bundle, Peter Dyck showed the children how to use their toothbrushes. Then they gathered up their treasures and started to leave. There was a long line forming, and the children were moving slowly. "Let's get going," Liese said impatiently. Sara knew the only reason she wanted to hurry was that David had already gone.

Sara stood on her tiptoes and looked over the crowd. Peter Dyck and his wife, Elfrieda, were giving each child a small bag as they went out the door. "Don't leave yet," Sara told Liese. "They're handing out something."

It was a brown bag and heavy for its size. Liese opened hers quickly and held up a shiny red apple. "Look," she exclaimed, "there's some candy, too. And raisins!"

Sara started to open hers, then she stopped and folded the top down again. There was something else she wanted to do with it.

Back in her room with her family, Sara had just as much fun opening the bundle a second time. She tried on her new skirt and sweater. "It's short," Mama said, lifting the edge of the skirt to examine the hem.

"Oh, let it," Marga said. "It's the style."

Mama let the skirt fall from her fingers and her mouth was firm. "I don't care what the style is. There's a hem there, and I'm going to lengthen it."

Sara held the skirt against her leg and added a hem's-length with her fingers. It still wasn't very long, she noticed happily, and took it off.

"What's this?" Marga said, picking up the brown bag.

"Oh, that's for Mama to put on my plate tonight," Sara said. She pulled her dish out from under the bed and set it on the table. Setting out the plate was an old Russian Mennonite custom, and Sara had set it out every Christmas since she could remember—except for the one at the Children's Home. In the morning she would say a poem and then find the goodies on her plate. It wasn't really a surprise like it should be, but it would be close enough. After all, she hadn't looked into the bag so she didn't know *exactly* what was there.

"It's been the best Christmas in my whole life," she said as she looked at the pile of things lying on her bed. "I really like it here."

"It's all right for now, but it won't last forever, you know," Franz said, smacking his fist into his other hand for emphasis. "I'm ready to get to Canada."

"Did you know the Rempels are leaving next week?" Mama asked.

Sara tensed and her eyes opened wide with surprise. "You mean Liese?"

"Yes, they're going to another camp at Fallingbostel for final processing before they can go to Canada."

"Oh, no!" Sara cried. "What's 'final processing,' anyway?"

"That's when Canadian officials give you medical tests and ask all kinds of questions to see if they will let you come to their country," Marga answered.

"Oh," Sara said in a flat voice. She folded up her new clothes and crawled into bed. She had thought all they needed was a letter from Uncle Jakob—now there was also this dreadful thing called *final processing*. She turned on her stomach and buried her face in the crook of her arm. A home for her was still a long way off.

CHAPTER 15

Spring came, and the tree in the front yard was full of white blossoms as it had been the day Sara had first seen it. But Sara missed Liese. One day after she had walked home from school alone and returned to her tiny blanketed room with nothing to do, she was particularly lonely.

"Why don't you take a walk?" her mother suggested.

"That's no fun by myself," Sara said, staring out the window.

"By the way, I got a letter today. Maybe you'd be interested in reading it." Mama handed her a white envelope.

Sara flopped down on the bed, propped herself on her elbows, and opened it. She scanned the letter for the signature—Liese's mother! "We did not pass the Canadian medical exam because I have tuberculosis. It has been very difficult for us, but we have decided to go to Paraguay. The loving God who has brought us out of the fire will go with us, so we have hope. Love, the Rempels."

Sara slowly folded the letter and stared out the window for a long time. Liese was not going to Canada. Her stomach felt hollow, and her shoulders were tense. Was it possible to be sick and not realize it? Perhaps she couldn't go to Canada even if Uncle Jakob *did* write.

Weeks passed and there was still no news of Uncle Jakob. Franz became increasingly impatient. "I'm going to find my own way to Canada," he announced one evening. "I can go as a miner or a logger and get my way paid by the government—after all, I'm eighteen now."

Mama's mouth quivered and she covered it with her hand. "If we can't find Uncle Jakob, you're our only hope for getting another sponsor. The few persons that don't have relatives of their own will only take a family if there's a man who can work."

Franz hung his head and cracked his knuckles. "I want to go to Canada," he said huskily. "Perhaps if I were there I could find Uncle Jakob."

"And if you couldn't?" Mama asked.

He didn't answer, and Sara could sense his struggle in the constant flexing of his arm muscle. Finally he got up and walked out of the room. Everyone was quiet.

At last Mama unfolded a flour sack and began cutting it to make a slip for Sara. Marga wound the heavy white sack string around her index finger and continued knitting a lacy collar for her sweater. Sara only watched. The click of the needles and repetitive swish of the scissors ordered the rhythm of her thoughts. Together—they had to stay together—they had to stay together—they had to stay. . . . The words formed a chant that filled her with determination. She got up and went out to find Franz.

Sara found him sitting under a tree in the front yard. She sat beside him, too afraid to say anything.

"What are you doing here?" he asked in a strained voice.

Sara's words tumbled out, "Couldn't you wait just a little longer to go to Canada? You can probably still go—just wait long enough to take us, too."

Franz picked up a fallen blossom and pulled it apart. "I'm tired of waiting," he said.

Sara was angry. "You think we're not tired?" she fumed. "Besides, you know you can go if you want to, and we don't."

Franz's eyes widened with astonishment. "Well!" he said, turning his head to look at her. "Since when did you become so spunky?"

"Since you've become so bullheaded!" she retorted.

Franz leaned back his head and suddenly laughed. "In that case I'd better slow down a bit. I'd hate to make you any more of a spitfire!"

Sara smiled. He wasn't the only one who had been surprised by her boldness.

Franz kept his word, and informed the MCC workers that he was willing to work for any sponsor who would take the whole family. Mama prayed. One by one their friends boarded the train for the refugee camp at Fallingbostel where the Canadian officials put them through final questioning and medical examinations before their entrance into Canada was approved.

Then the letter came. "From Canada, from Canada!" Franz shouted as he threw back the blanket door. Mama took it, and Sara could see her eyes fill with tears. "Uncle Jakob," she said softly. "He wants us to come to Canada. God has provided," Mamma said with tears running down her cheeks.

"One step closer," Sara thought. Next was Fallingbostel and the medical exam.

The refugee camp at Fallingbostel was beautiful. The two-story stone buildings that had been an army training center were surrounded by a forest of evergreen trees. And although there were thousands of refugees from many countries, the Mennonites lived in one section of the camp secluded from the other refugees by the lovely trees. The barracks had been built for sleeping, so there was a small room for each family. Up the stairs in long attic rooms, the people gathered for school and evening services.

School! It was different from any Sara had experienced. When Herr Wiebe finished taking the roll the first day, he walked around to the front of the desk, pushed his glasses up on his nose, and folded his hands across his chest. "Now," he said, "we don't have many books yet, although we did manage to get some scraps of paper from a print shop. But I think there are a lot of things we can learn anyway. As you know, we are all refugees— how many of you know what a refugee is?"

Sara looked down at her feet—"You take our food . . . Ignorant . . . We don't want you." The words raced through her mind. No one answered.

"A refugee is a person who has to flee from his country because of persecution. How many of you had to flee from your country?" Sara's mind went back over the long trek, and slowly raised her hand—but only as high as her shoulder.

"Even here in Germany we are still without a home. All of your parents are trying to find homes. You probably hear them talking about Canada and Paraguay. So today I thought we would spend some time talking about these countries." Herr Wiebe unfolded a big sheet of paper and held it up for everyone to see. Sara held her breath. The last map she'd seen hung on their schoolroom wall in Russia, and she had been too young to understand it then.

Herr Wiebe pointed to Russia and showed how they had gone to Poland on the long trek and then on to Germany. He showed them where they were now—Gronau, a tiny dot right beside the boundary line of Holland. Then the great Atlantic Ocean that separated them from Canada, and way at the bottom of the map, Paraguay.

He told them about the prairies of Canada which were very much like their own Russia, only colder in winter. Sara learned that there truly were cars in Canada and that most families had one. And that the black soil of the prairies had provided rich crops of wheat and vast grazing lands for the Russian Mennonites who had gone to Canada nearly seventy years before.

She learned about the colonies in Paraguay, built ten years earlier by Mennonites from Russia. And she listened as Herr Wiebe told them how the wilderness had been cleared by the pioneers while they lived in mud huts and ate and drank strange foods such as manioc and yerba maté. She heard about the primitive culture of the native Indians, and the hard quebracho wood that grew in the thick jungle. For the first time she felt proud to be a refugee.

At supper that night Sara said, "We learned about Canada and Paraguay today."

"Canada is the place to go," Franz said decidedly.

"Liese is in Paraguay," Sara said, thinking about the medical exam.

She probably lives in a mud hut, too," Franz said scornfully.

"They had no choice," Mama reminded him.

"Well, in Canada they have nice houses and cars and rich soil. Besides, Paraguay is always hot."

Sara stirred the chunks of meat gravy on her plate. She knew Franz wanted to go to Canada. Uncle Jakob had invited them. But something about the way Franz said it made her stomach ache.

Sara was so busy learning that she didn't even realize that she was comfortable in a new school without Liese. Herr Wiebe made her feel like she belonged—something he did for all the children. He told them about the tiny atom that had the power to propel a huge ship. He unlocked the mysteries of the planets and stars as they moved in orderly motion through the sky. And he captured beautiful thoughts in lilting words as he quoted poetry. Sara sat on the edge of her bench with wide-open eyes and listened. It was as if he were taking the chaotic pieces of the world and placing them into an interlocking puzzle.

"I have news for you," Herr Wiebe said one morning. "Our family has received a permit from the Canadian Immigration Office." Sara sat up straight and swung her foot nervously. The room was quiet. "We will be leaving in a few days, so I have something special for you today." He picked up a large piece of cardboard, propped it against the wall, and read the poem that was printed on it:

IN REMEMBRANCE
Dear Children, we can see at last
What is to be our native land
For far away beyond the haze
Appears to us the hoped-for place
To all of you I'd like to say,
These truths lock in your heart today:

Be full of joy in all your days
If good or trouble come your way.
For cheerfulness makes burdens light
And makes another's sad heart bright.

Have upright ways and honest, too,
But not for show must you be true
For nothing good will here arise
From acting false and living lies.

Be always helpful to your friends
For with good works a prayer ascends
The things we do as well as say
Through all eternity remain.

In remembrance and to be taken to heart
by the students of the seventh and eighth grades
of the Mennonite School in Fallingbostel.

> Written July 27, 1948.
> Your teacher,
> Johann Wiebe.

Sara picked up her pencil as Herr Wiebe handed her a sheet of white paper. She rubbed it smooth and began writing, forming each letter with extra care. Already she had decided that she would keep it forever.

School wasn't the same now that Herr Wiebe was on his way to Canada. Sara lay on her bed with her head in her hands. Would she ever get to Canada? They had waited for months. . . .

"Tomorrow!" Franz shouted as he pushed the door open. "We can take our medical tests tomorrow! Can you believe it? One step closer to Canada!"

"What if we don't make it?" Marga asked as she entered the room behind him.

"Then we don't get to Canada," Franz said. "But we'd better make it." His voice was adamant.

Sara looked at him, then buried her face in her pillow. What if they didn't.

CHAPTER 16

Sara climbed the attic steps behind her mother and set her box behind the people who had already gathered for worship. Evening services would start any minute now. In front of them, a young girl huddled against her mother, sobbing.

"They had their medical exam today," the woman beside them whispered, "and they didn't pass—trachoma, I think."

"What's trachoma?" Sara asked her mother.

"An eye disease," Mama answered.

Sara blinked hard and folded her arms tightly against her body. Would that be how it would be for her tomorrow night? Her eyes blurred and her head throbbed. The chorale melodies drifted up and down, an undercurrent of sound that left Sara untouched and frozen.

"I have my medical exam tomorrow,"—the words spoken by an old woman cut through Sara's stupor. The woman smoothed her black head scarf, and tears rolled down her wrinkled face. Her voice choked with emotion. "Pray for me."

"Could God really make a difference?" Sara wondered later as she lay awake worrying. And if he could, why didn't he let everyone pass—like the girl with trachoma? She rolled on her side and stared into the darkness. She understood about as much as she could see—only gray shapes in the black room. "God," she whispered, "if you can hear me now, please listen. I've been trying to grow up and make things happen for myself, but there's nothing I can do about this medical exam. Please take care of it for me."

The sun was streaming in the window when Sara awoke the next morning. She tried to dress quickly, but everything went wrong. The tooth of her comb broke when she tried to get a tangle out of her hair. She dripped porridge on her dress and skinned her leg on the top bunk while she was making her bed. Then when she was pouring water from the pitcher to wash her face, she slopped it all over the table. It was one thing too much. She was sure now that she was too clumsy to ever be declared medically fit for Canada. Maybe her eyes were bad; maybe that's why she was so clumsy. Maybe she had trachoma. Maybe she'd had it a long time and didn't even know about it. She rubbed her eyes until they hurt. Now she was sure—she had trachoma, and she would never be able to go to Canada.

At eight-thirty Sara followed her family down the sidewalk. Franz was upset that she walked so slowly and Marga kept telling her not to act so foolish. Mama didn't say anything.

They were early enough so that only one family had arrived ahead of them. Sara sat down so stiffly she could feel her hip bones sharp against the wooden seat. One horrible minute after another passed while she waited for her name to be called. She was still sitting long after Franz, Marga, and Mama had all been called. Her eyes watered, and she blinked nervously and rubbed them with her fist.

"Sara Friesen," a nurse called out. Sara responded to orders like a robot—weight, height, blood tests, X-rays. "You'll have to wait at least five days to find out about the tests," the nurse said when she was finished. "We'll make an appointment with the doctor next week sometime. How about Wednesday?"

Next Wednesday? Sara clenched her hands and swallowed hard. That seemed like forever. A whole week to think about facing a horrible medical examiner who could punch and poke and with one word decide whether or not she could go to Canada. She felt the stuffiness of the room closing in on her, and she rushed out of the room, past her waiting family, and out the door.

The chill fall air sent goose bumps along her arms and made the hair stand straight up. She folded her arms and rubbed her hands back and forth over them, trying to keep warm. She would probably never get to Canada. What if she were the only person in the whole family who didn't pass the exam? What if she spoiled it for all of them? She kicked at a stone and held her arms tight against her body. What if they would go anyway and just leave her behind? Her throat tightened, and tears started running down her cheeks. She didn't want to see the doctor. She didn't want to go back on Wednesday. She was sick of trying to get to Canada.

As she shuffled along, her foot hit a pinecone and sent it rolling. She sat down, picked it up, and scraped it slowly over the palm of her hand. It felt smooth and sent a dull tingle through her hand. She held it up and pushed at the individual scales, then started digging with it in the damp soil. Several scales broke off, and she covered them with dirt and patted it firmly. "Perhaps it will be a tree someday," she thought. She imagined it pushing up through the ground, a tiny twig of green, then growing taller each year until it spread its branches to cover the ground where she was sitting.

She clawed at the soil and uncovered the scales again. She didn't want to keep them in that dark place under the cold earth. The unknown of her own future left her more tense than the crisp air. Even the air raid siren had not made her as afraid as this medical exam. She picked up the seeds, turned them over in her hand, and put them back into the ground. Only the dark earth could make them germinate and grow. The only way she could get to Canada was to go through the exam.

She drew up her legs and propped her chin on her knees. "I *will* take the exam," she said aloud, packing the ground with a determined push of her hand. The damp earth responded to the sudden pressure, and she recognized her strength in the shape of her palm on the black ground.

She sat quietly, staring at the row of stately pine trees. Finally she stood up and brushed herself off. B-r-r-r! It was getting colder.

"Where in the world have you been?" Marga yelled, running up to her. "We've been looking all over."

Sara looked down and kicked at a pinecone. "Just sitting here thinking," she said.

"About what?" Marga asked, relaxing a little.

Sara looked at Marga, and her eyes squinted. "What if I don't pass the exam?" she said with more force than she had intended.

Marga straightened with surprise. "Well, we'd probably go to Paraguay," she said.

"You wouldn't leave me behind?" Sara asked, and her voice trembled.

"No!" Marga said with feeling. "Our family is staying together. Come on, let's go talk to Mama about it." She took Sara's hand and they ran back to their room.

They were just in time for dinner, and the walk had made Sara hungry. The liver sausage on her plate surrounded by piles of potato and turnip looked good, and she ate eagerly.

"Mama," Marga asked, "what if one of us doesn't pass the exam?"

Sara looked at Franz intently. His eyes stayed fixed on his plate as he chewed a piece of sausage.

"We'd probably go to Paraguay," Mama said, matter-of-factly.

Franz looked at Mama for a long time. "Yes," he said, "we need to stay together. Besides, Sara wouldn't let me do anything else." And he winked at her.

Sara felt like jumping up and hugging him, she was so happy. But she didn't. "I'm going to see the doctor and try to get to Canada," she announced instead.

"You mean you thought about not taking the exam?" Franz said with alarm.

Sara bowed her head and fiddled with her fork. "I was afraid," she said softly. Then she looked straight at Franz. "I still am afraid, but I'm going anyway."

The following Wednesday, at nine o'clock, Sara sat on the examination table taking her medical exam. "Are you scared?" the doctor asked as he took his stethoscope out of his ears and dropped the end into his pocket. "You're heart's pumping pretty fast in there."

The doctor looked into her eyes, pulled down the lower lid, and told her to roll her eyes. Sara held her breath and pressed her hands hard against the table. "They look fine," the doctor said.

Fine? Sara's heart beat even faster, and she kicked her foot against the table in excitement.

The doctor picked up a folder and flipped through the papers inside. "You're OK," he said, giving her a pat on the shoulder. "You can go to Canada."

Sara jumped off the table and followed the nurse out the door. Mama, Marga, and Franz were all waiting for her. "I made it," she said, grabbing her mother's arm. "I can go to Canada!" She laughed and jumped, and tears streamed down her face.

Marga hugged her, and Franz clasped his hands above his head in excitement. "We can all go!" he yelled.

"Everyone of us passed," Mama explained, putting her free hand on Sara's. "Truly God has been with us." And she wept.

As they walked home, Sara could see a lone pine tree across the campgrounds. Suddenly her stomach tightened. She was back at another tree, all alone except for Liese and one small potato. But there had been people who cared—the Red Cross nurse with the sweet marmalade; the woman on the train with the two small children; Metchthild and Gudrun, even though they were reluctant at first; Sister Katrina and all the workers at the Children's Home; then there was the Dutch woman near Gronau who gave her food in exchange for knitting; and all the workers in the refugee camps who had provided her food and a place to stay.

God *had* taken care of her. She looked at the tree again, unafraid.

FALLINGBOSTEL

HOLLAND

HATTO

GRONAU

FRANKFURT

NUREMBERG

SARAS' TREK

ANSBACH

Sara's Journeys

Steinfeld, Russia
    Left in October of 1943
Wulka, Poland (Wartegau)
    Arrived in spring of 1944 - January 1945
Ansbach, Germany (Children's Home)
    Stayed until fall of 1945
Hattorf, Germany
    Late 1945-early 1946
    Father died in January 1946
Gronau, Germany (MCC Refugee camps)
    1946-48
Fallingbostel, Germany (processing camp)
    Fall 1948
Canada, November 1948

Florence Schloneger was born on a Kansas farm about the time Sara's trek was nearing its end. As a young girl, she read *Henry's Red Sea* by Barbara Smucker and was impressed with the suffering and strength of the Mennonite refugees during World War II.

Although *Sara's Trek* is fiction, most of the incidents grow out of real-life experiences. Several years ago while she and her husband were both students at Associated Mennonite Biblical Seminaries, Florence enjoyed the friendship of a student who had been a refugee girl. She knew then that she wanted to write the story.

Florence and her husband, Weldon, live in Columbus, Ohio. They have two sons, Matthew and Timothy.